THE UNOFFICIAL

HOLY BIBLE

FOR

MINECRAFTERS

NEW TESTAMENT

THE UNOFFICIAL
HOLY BIBLE
FOR
MINECRAFTERS
NEW TESTAMENT

Stories from the Bible Told Block by Block

⟨ CHRISTOPHER MIKO AND GARRETT ROMINES ⟩

SKY PONY PRESS
NEW YORK

Copyright © 2016 by Christopher Miko and Garrett Romines

Sky Pony Press books may be purchased in bulk at special discounts for sales promotion, corporate gifts, fund-raising, or educational purposes. Special editions can also be created to specifications. For details, contact the Special Sales Department, Sky Pony Press, 307 West 36th Street, 11th Floor, New York, NY 10018 or info@skyhorsepublishing.com.

Sky Pony® is a registered trademark of Skyhorse Publishing, Inc.®, a Delaware corporation.

Minecraft® is a registered trademark of Notch Development AB. The Minecraft game is copyright © Mojang AB.

Visit our website at www.skyhorsepublishing.com.

10 9 8 7 6 5 4 3

Library of Congress Cataloging-in-Publication Data is available on file.

Cover design by Brian Peterson
Cover photos by Christopher Miko

ISBN: 978-1-5107-0182-3
Ebook ISBN: 978-1-5107-1105-1

Printed in China

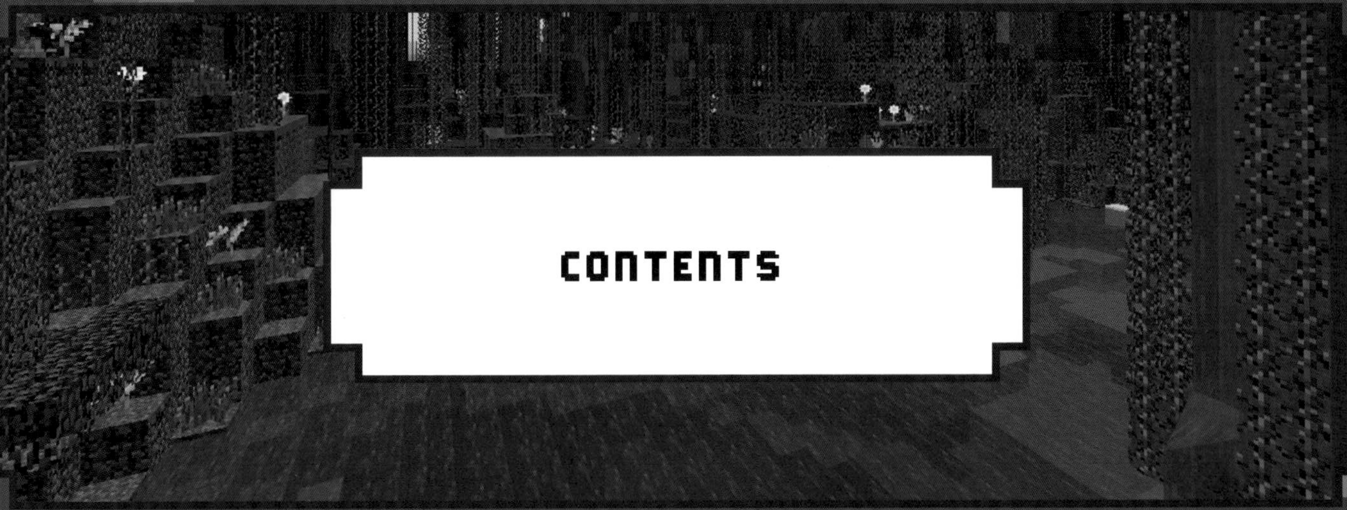

CONTENTS

DEDICATION

I WOULD LIKE TO DEDICATE THIS BOOK to my loving wife Lindsey. She endured me making it during the first year of our marriage. God bless her.

—Chris

I give glory to God in the highest praise for his blessings upon me, and to my friend and coauthor Chris Miko.

—Garrett

FOREWORD

WE ARE ALL GOD-SEEKING PEOPLE from the time we are born. The Bible is God's story about Himself and His relationship with human beings. Children who wish to learn more about the Bible and about God are blessed children! Bible stories inspire young people to grow in ways beyond their imagination. They will use these stories to become wonderful human beings.

As parents, it can be difficult to get children to read the Bible. In *The Unofficial Holy Bible for Minecrafters*, children will engage the Bible in a way that they enjoy. God's Creation story is full of profound life lessons. There are many answers in this book to challenges children may be facing in their own lives. Kids will learn from these stories how to be strong and courageous. Jesus faced bullies and had allies. He experienced peer-pressure and had to become comfortable with His identity as the Son of God. The Bible is an essential part of knowing and learning about our true selves. Scripture provides a blueprint and structure for how to live a wonderful life.

The colorful illustrations in this marvelous work bring biblical characters to life in a way far beyond what I could have ever imagined having available to me as a child. The illustrations were created in the video game Minecraft and provide a unique setting for the stories. This also further teaches parents to embrace the new world of youth and gaming and learn how it can be used as a resource in education overall.

I encourage the Christian community to share this book with their loved ones and to facilitate further discussion about God and the Bible in their homes and communities. This book definitely makes it more fun!

TERRY A. SMITH,
Lead Pastor, The Life Christian Church

LETTER TO PARENTS

DEAR PARENTS,

If your child is one of the mass millions who enjoys playing Minecraft and you want to encourage your child to learn more and take a stronger interest in reading the Bible, *The Unofficial Holy Bible for Minecrafters* provides an excellent opportunity to introduce Bible stories in a fun and exciting way.

This beautifully illustrated book, full of over 250 amazing images will enable the child not to just read the Bible stories but to understand them in a way he or she can incorporate the messages into everyday decision-making.

With these stories, children will explore competency, autonomy, and self-identity from a new perspective. The Minecraft game gives players the opportunity to be creative, solve problems, and interact. In many ways, that is what we want our kids to do with the Bible stories. Bible stories serve to teach our children about how God interacts in the world and how He would want us to interact in the world.

The Unofficial Holy Bible for Minecrafters uses the world of Minecraft to capture the imagination of children and is cutting edge. It joins a long line of contemporary methods used to introduce the Bible to children.

Sincerely,
Rev. Dr. Wanda M. Lundry

BIRTH OF JOHN THE BAPTIST

Yay, the New Testament!

IN THE TIME OF HEROD, THE KING OF JUDEA, THE ROMANS RULED ALL THE KNOWN WORLD.

THOUGH SUBJECTS TO ROME, THE PEOPLE OF ISRAEL STILL HELD FAITH THAT THE MESSIAH WOULD COME.

ONE OF THESE BELIEVERS WAS A PRIEST NAMED ZECHARIAH.

ZECHARIAH AND HIS WIFE ELIZABETH WERE RIGHTEOUS IN THE SIGHT OF THE LORD.

ZECHARIAH AND ELIZABETH ASKED ONLY ONE THING FROM GOD: TO GIVE THEM A CHILD.

YEARS PASSED AND ZECHARIAH AND ELIZABETH GREW OLD, YET THEY HAD NOT BEEN BLESSED WITH A CHILD.

We have decided that you, Zechariah, should carry out the prayers.

This is a great honor. Thank you.

You have earned it.

ONE DAY, ZECHARIAH WAS CHOSEN TO GO INTO THE TEMPLE OF THE LORD AND BURN INCENSE.

I am so nervous!

I am so proud of you. There is no finer man to give praise to God.

ZECHARIAH PREPARED HIMSELF FOR THIS SACRED DUTY. HE DID NOT KNOW THAT GOD HAD A GREATER PURPOSE FOR HIM THAT DAY.

THE PEOPLE GATHERED OUTSIDE THE TEMPLE TO PRAY WHILE ZECHARIAH ENTERED.

SOON AFTER HE'D LIT THE INCENSE ON A CANDLE, AN ANGEL OF THE LORD APPEARED BEFORE ZECHARIAH.

Do not be afraid, for I am here with good tidings.

WHEN ZECHARIAH SAW THE ANGEL HE BECAME AFRAID, AND BOWED LOW TO AVERT HIS EYES.

Your prayers have been heard. Your wife will soon have a son.

He will be the voice that calls out from the wilderness to make ready the people, for the Lord is coming!

I don't believe you. I am old and so is my wife.

ZECHARIAH DID NOT BELIEVE THEY WOULD BEAR A CHILD.

You do not believe God can grant what he says? For this, you will be silent until the day the child is born!

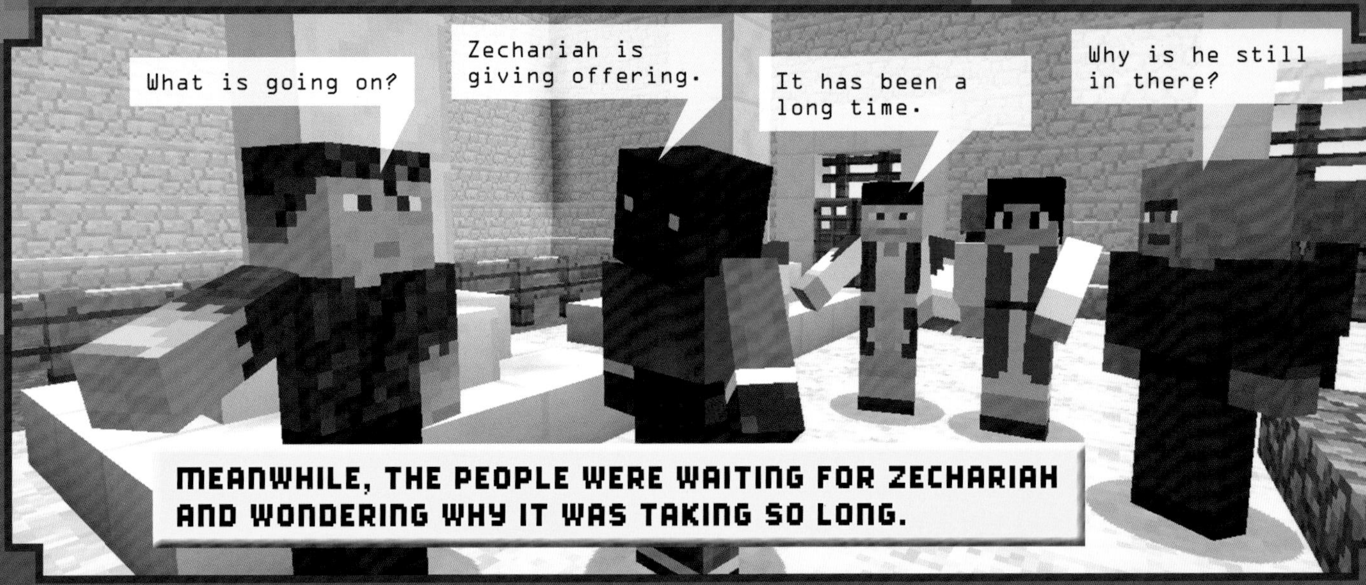
What is going on?
Zechariah is giving offering.
It has been a long time.
Why is he still in there?
MEANWHILE, THE PEOPLE WERE WAITING FOR ZECHARIAH AND WONDERING WHY IT WAS TAKING SO LONG.

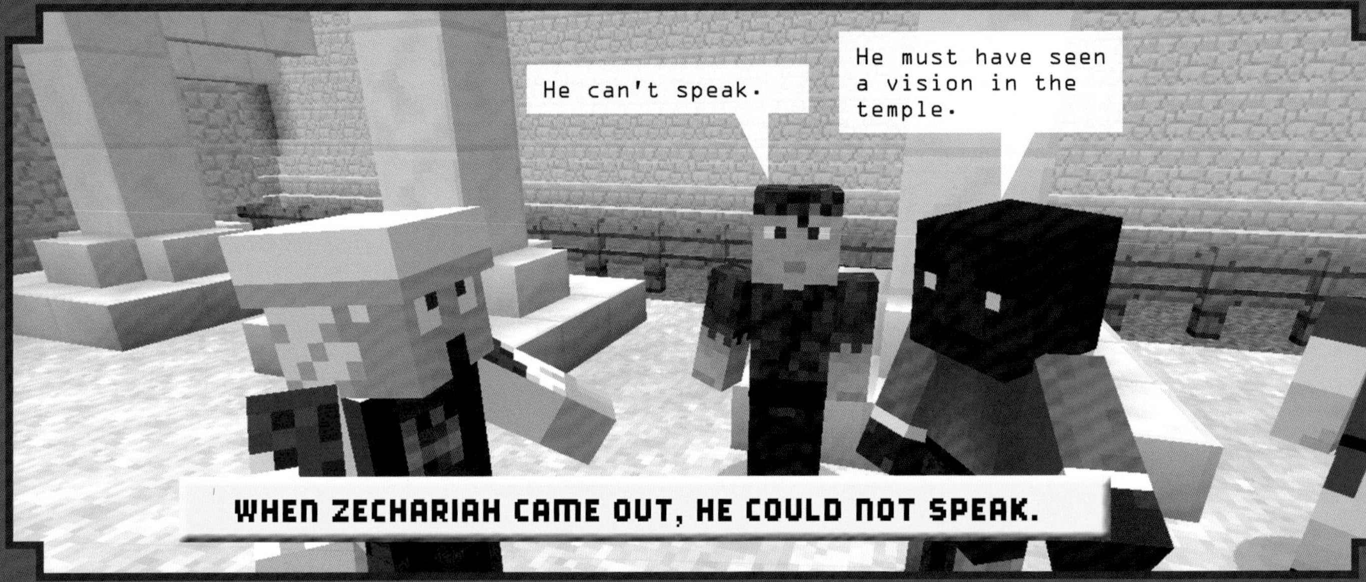
He can't speak.
He must have seen a vision in the temple.
WHEN ZECHARIAH CAME OUT, HE COULD NOT SPEAK.

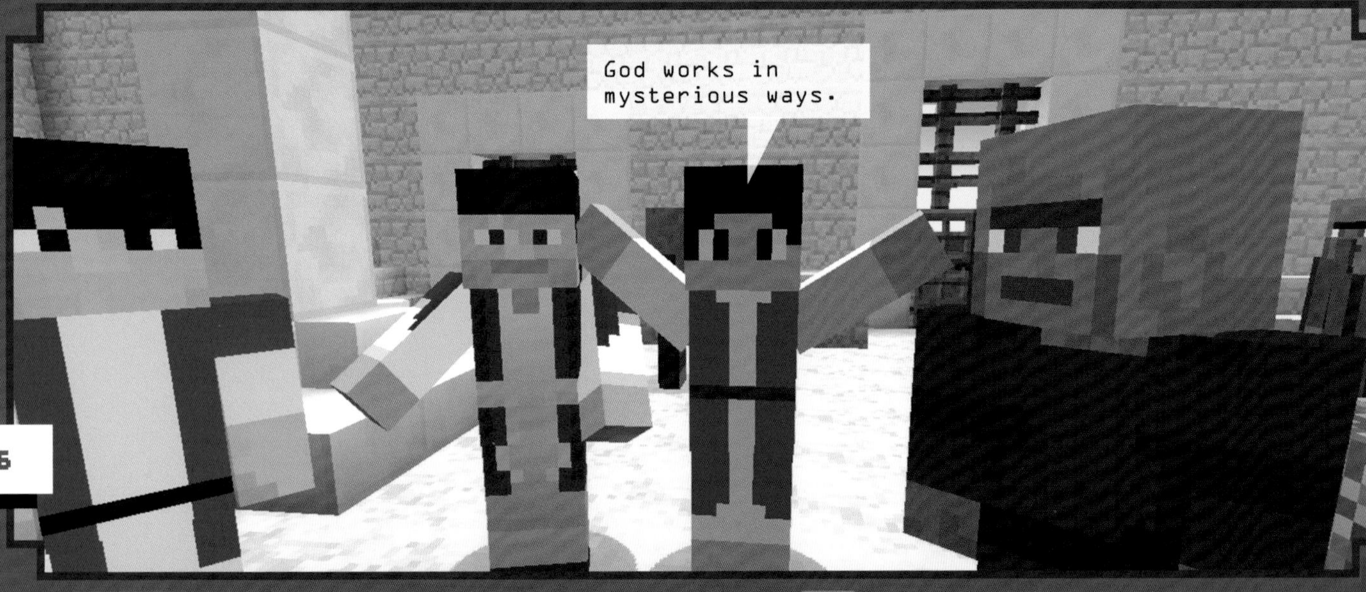
God works in mysterious ways.

You may not be able to speak, but God has kept his promise.

ZECHARIAH RETURNED HOME AND TRIED TO EXPLAIN WHAT HAPPENED TO HIS WIFE BUT HE COULD NOT SPEAK. IN TIME, ELIZABETH LEARNED SHE WAS WITH CHILD, AS GOD SAID SHE WOULD.

FOR FIVE MONTHS, ELIZABETH REMAINED IN SECLUSION. THERE SHE PRAYED AND DEDICATED HERSELF TO THE LORD.

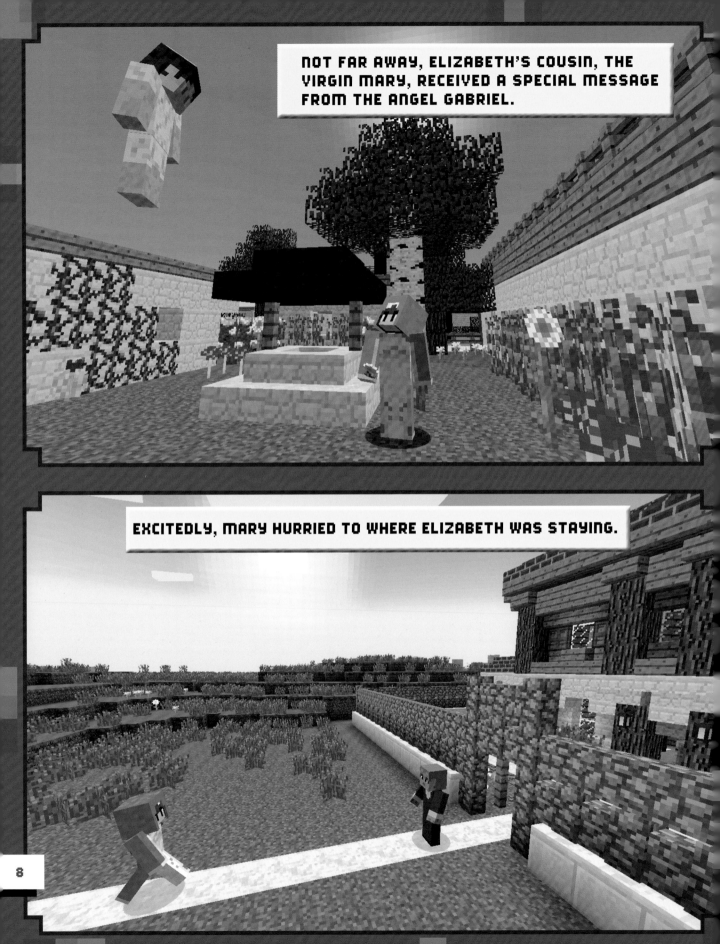

NOT FAR AWAY, ELIZABETH'S COUSIN, THE VIRGIN MARY, RECEIVED A SPECIAL MESSAGE FROM THE ANGEL GABRIEL.

EXCITEDLY, MARY HURRIED TO WHERE ELIZABETH WAS STAYING.

WHEN ELIZABETH HUGGED MARY, HER BABY ROLLED IN HER WOMB.

My child jumps for joy and I feel the Holy Spirit when I see you, Mary. How are you?

An angel came to me and told me I am with child from the Holy Spirit.

Blessed are you among women! But why am I so favored that the mother of the Lord should come to me?

I have come to stay with you until the birth of your son.

WHEN IT WAS TIME FOR ELIZABETH TO GIVE BIRTH, SHE HAD A SON.

No, he is to be named John.

THEY WERE GOING TO NAME THE BOY AFTER HIS FATHER, BUT ELIZABETH SPOKE UP.

There is no one in your family that has that name.

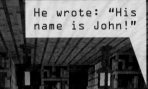

He wrote: "His name is John!"

THEY LOOKED AT ZECHARIAH AS HE MOTIONED TO THE WRITING TABLET AND GRABBED A STYLUS.

Praise the Lord. His name is John.

FINALLY, ZECHARIAH'S MOUTH OPENED, AND HE WAS ABLE TO SPEAK.

It's a miracle.

This is only the beginning.

ALL THE NEIGHBORS SAID THAT THE BABY WOULD BE A GREAT PROPHET.

THE CHILD GREW AND BECAME STRONG IN SPIRIT, AS HE LIVED IN THE
WILDERNESS UNTIL HE APPEARED PUBLICLY TO ISRAEL AS AN ADULT.

11

THE BIRTH OF CHRIST

Here comes your son!

MARY WAS PLEDGED TO BE MARRIED TO JOSEPH, BUT BEFORE THEY CAME TO-GETHER, SHE WAS FOUND TO BE WITH CHILD THROUGH THE HOLY SPIRIT. JOSEPH, HER HUSBAND, DID NOT WANT TO EXPOSE HER TO PUBLIC DISGRACE. HE HAD IN MIND TO DIVORCE HER QUIETLY.

THE ANGEL OF THE LORD APPEARED TO JOSEPH IN A DREAM. THE ANGEL GABRIEL TOLD JOSEPH TO TAKE MARY AS HIS WIFE.

JOSEPH JOURNEYED TO REGISTER WITH MARY, WHO WAS PLEDGED TO BE MARRIED TO HIM AND WAS EXPECTING A CHILD.

WHEN JOSEPH AND MARY TRIED TO FIND LODGING IN BETHLEHEM, THERE WAS NO PLACE FOR THEM BECAUSE THE INN WAS ALREADY FULL. THEY ENDED UP SPENDING THE NIGHT IN A STABLE, A PLACE WHERE ANIMALS WERE KEPT.

Sir, I know you have said that you are full, but my wife is expecting.

Inn
No Place
Like Home

The best I can do is my stable.

THE TIME CAME FOR THE BABY TO BE BORN, AND MARY GAVE BIRTH TO A SON. SHE WRAPPED HIM IN CLOTH AND PLACED HIM IN A MANGER. AS GOD INSTRUCTED, JOSEPH NAMED THE CHILD.

Do not be afraid. I bring you good news. Today in the town of David, a Savior has been born to you; he is the Messiah, the Lord. This will be a sign to you: you will find a baby wrapped in cloths and lying in a manger.

THERE WERE SHEPHERDS LIVING OUT IN THE FIELDS NEARBY. AN ANGEL OF THE LORD APPEARED TO THEM AS THE GLORY OF THE LORD SHONE AROUND THEM.

Could it be that this great miracle has happened?

Imagine! The Messiah has come. We must give praise.

THE ANGEL LEFT AND RETURNED TO HEAVEN.

Believe me, God's deliverance for man has come. Praise the Lord.

THE SHEPHERDS SPREAD THE WORD CONCERNING WHAT THEY HAD BEEN TOLD ABOUT THE CHILD. ALL WHO HEARD IT WERE AMAZED AT WHAT THE SHEPHERDS SAID TO THEM.

AFTER THE BIRTH OF JESUS, A STAR APPEARED. THREE WISE MEN SET OUT TO FOLLOW THE STAR AND MADE THEIR WAY TOWARD JERUSALEM TO ASK WHERE THEY COULD FIND THIS MIRACLE. ONCE THEY ARRIVED IN JERUSALEM, THEY WERE TOLD THAT THEY WOULD FIND THE BABY IN BETHLEHEM. SO ONWARD THEY MADE THEIR PILGRIMAGE WITH THE STAR AHEAD OF THEM, UNTIL IT STOPPED ABOVE THE PLACE WHERE THE CHILD LAY.

I give praise to the heavens above to have been able to see this miracle with my own eyes.

THE THREE WISE MEN FOUND THE BABY JESUS WITH HIS MOTHER. THEY BOWED AND WORSHIPED HIM.

THE WISE MEN BEGAN THE JOURNEY HOME TO SPREAD THE WORD OF THE NEWBORN CHILD.

THE ESCAPE TO EGYPT

Get up, take the child and his mother and escape to Egypt. Stay there until I tell you, for Herod is going to search for the child.

WHEN THE THREE WISE MEN HAD GONE, AN ANGEL OF THE LORD APPEARED TO JOSEPH IN A DREAM.

HASTILY, JOSEPH READIED THEIR BELONGINGS AND TOOK THE CHILD AND HIS MOTHER DURING THE NIGHT TO EGYPT.

WHEN KING HEROD REALIZED THAT THE WISE MEN WOULD NOT HELP HIM GET JESUS, HE THREW A TANTRUM AND TOOK HIS ANGER OUT ON THE PEOPLE.

It's not fair, I am King. I should get what I want.

THIS FULFILLED THE PROPHECY OF JEREMIAH.

HEROD SENT HIS TROOPS INTO EVERY HOUSE LOOKING FOR BABY JESUS, BUT THEY DID NOT FIND HIM.

SHORTLY AFTER JESUS WAS TAKEN TO EGYPT, HEROD DIED.

ONCE AGAIN, AN ANGEL OF THE LORD APPEARED TO JOSEPH IN A DREAM.

Get up, take the child and his mother and go to the land of Israel, for those who were trying to take the child are gone.

SO WAS FULFILLED WHAT THE LORD HAD SAID THROUGH THE PROPHET: "OUT OF EGYPT I CALLED MY SON."

ONCE AGAIN, JOSEPH PACKED THEIR THINGS AND TOOK HIS FAMILY TO THE LAND OF ISRAEL.

Welcome to sunny Egypt!

WHEN JOSEPH AND MARY HEARD THAT HEROD'S SON ARCHELAUS WAS REIGNING IN JUDEA, JOSEPH WAS AFRAID.

We must find another place to live.

If Herod wanted the child, would his evil son want less?

JOSEPH AND MARY WITHDREW TO THE DISTRICT OF GALILEE AND MOVED INTO THE TOWN OF NAZARETH. THIS, ONCE AGAIN, FULFILLED THE WORDS OF THE PROPHETS.

WHEN THE TIME CAME FOR THE PURIFICATION RITES REQUIRED BY THE LAW OF MOSES, JOSEPH AND MARY TOOK JESUS TO JERUSALEM TO PRESENT HIM TO THE LORD.

THERE WAS A MAN IN JERUSALEM NAMED SIMEON WHO WAS RIGHTEOUS AND DEVOUT. HE WAS WAITING FOR THE COMING OF THE MESSIAH.

Still waiting for the Messiah, Simeon? He better come soon. You are really getting old.

That I am, my friend.

THE HOLY SPIRIT HAD REVEALED TO SIMEON THAT HE WOULD NOT DIE BEFORE HE HAD SEEN THE LORD'S MESSIAH.

MOVED BY THE HOLY SPIRIT, SIMEON WENT INTO THE TEMPLE COURTS, NOT KNOWING WHY OR WHAT HE WAS LOOKING TO FIND.

WHEN THE PARENTS BROUGHT IN THE CHILD, JESUS, TO PERFORM HIS RITES, SIMEON SAW JESUS. THE HOLY SPIRIT TOLD HIM THAT JESUS WAS THE MESSIAH. UNABLE TO CONTROL HIS EXCITEMENT, SIMEON RAN UP TO JESUS.

SIMEON CRIED AND HUGGED JESUS.

Sovereign Lord, as you have promised, my eyes have seen your salvation. A light for revelation to the Gentiles, and the glory of your people Israel. I have seen the Lord, I can now go to him in peace knowing that the prophecies have been fulfilled.

How did he know?

It is proclaimed aloud. He is the Messiah.

THE CHILD'S FATHER AND MOTHER MARVELED AT WHAT WAS SAID ABOUT JESUS.

This child is destined to cause the rising of many to the Lord. All will reveal their hearts to him, the wicked and the righteous.

SIMEON THEN TURNED TO MARY, MOTHER OF JESUS, AND ADDRESSED HER.

ANOTHER PROPHET, ANNA, THE DAUGHTER OF PENUEL, ALSO KEPT VIGIL FOR THE SAVIOR. SHE NEVER LEFT THE TEMPLE AND WORSHIPED NIGHT AND DAY.

SHE HAPPENED TO COME TO THEM AT THE VERY MOMENT SIMEON SPOKE ABOUT JESUS. SHE GAVE THANKS TO GOD AND SAID THE CHILD WOULD BRING REDEMPTION.

This is the son of God, the Messiah, spoken of in prophecy!

WHEN JOSEPH AND MARY HAD DONE EVERYTHING REQUIRED BY THE LAW OF THE LORD, THEY RETURNED TO GALILEE AND THEIR HOME TO RAISE JESUS.

THE CHILD JESUS GREW AND BECAME STRONG: HE WAS FILLED WITH WISDOM, AND THE GRACE OF GOD WAS WITHIN HIM.

THE BOY JESUS AT THE TEMPLE

Even as a boy, He is starting to do amazing things.

EVERY YEAR, JESUS' PARENTS TRAVELED TO JERUSALEM FOR THE FESTIVAL OF THE PASSOVER. JESUS WAS TWELVE YEARS OLD ON THIS OCCASION.

AFTER THE FESTIVAL, WHILE JESUS' PARENTS WERE GATHERING THEIR THINGS, THE YOUNG BOY WENT OUT TO THE TEMPLE ON HIS OWN.

JOSEPH AND MARY WERE SO BUSY PREPARING TO LEAVE, AND THERE WERE SO MANY MEMBERS IN THE TRAVELING PARTY, THEY DID NOT NOTICE JESUS WASN'T WITH THEM.

Mary, the boy is far more capable than you or I. He is probably in the back with the other kids.

I haven't seen Jesus in a while!

AS THE CARAVAN LEFT THE CITY GATES, JOSEPH AND MARY HAD A MOMENT TO TAKE STOCK.

33

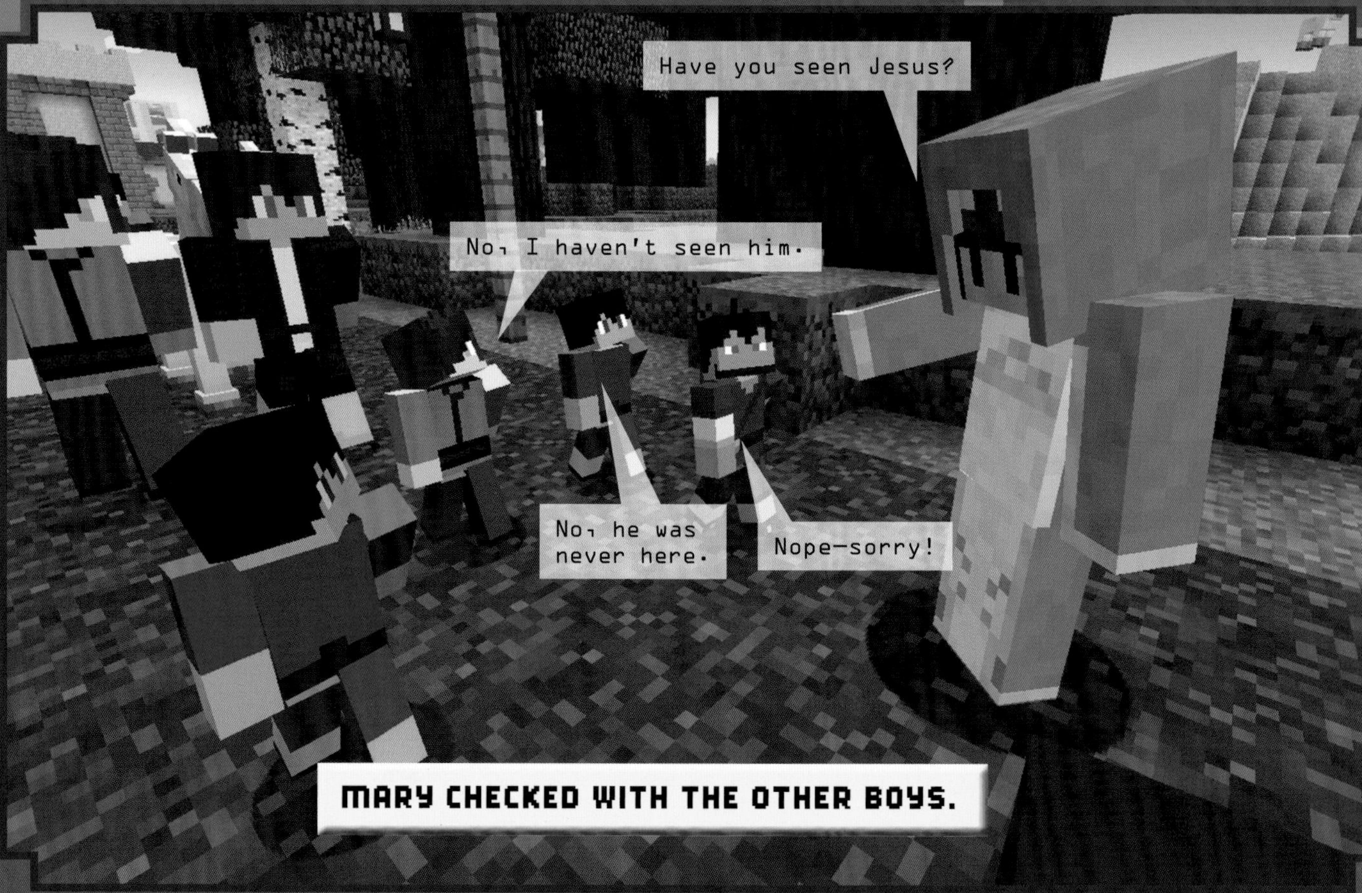
Have you seen Jesus?
No, I haven't seen him.
No, he was never here.
Nope—sorry!
MARY CHECKED WITH THE OTHER BOYS.

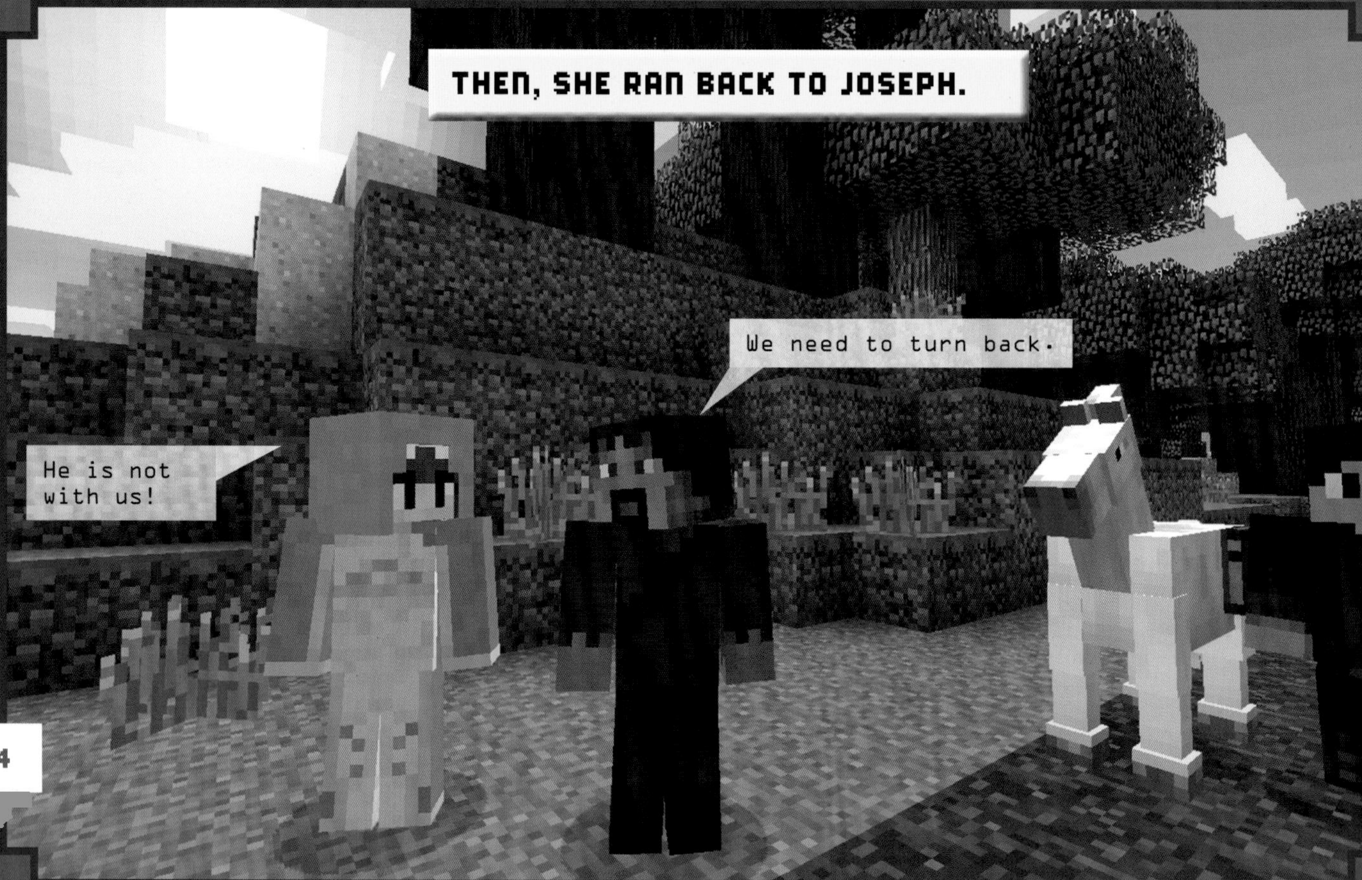
THEN, SHE RAN BACK TO JOSEPH.
He is not with us!
We need to turn back.

LEAVING THE CARAVAN, THEY TURNED BACK AND WENT TO JERUSALEM.

FOR THREE DAYS, MARY AND JOSEPH SEARCHED FOR JESUS.

We are looking for our son. He is twelve.

Excuse me, have you seen our son?

You have to go to the temple and hear this young man speak.

FINALLY, THEY OVERHEAD A MAN WHO WAS MARVELLING AT SOMETHING HE HAD JUST SEEN.

He speaks with the authority of God. This boy Jesus is far beyond anything I have ever heard or seen.

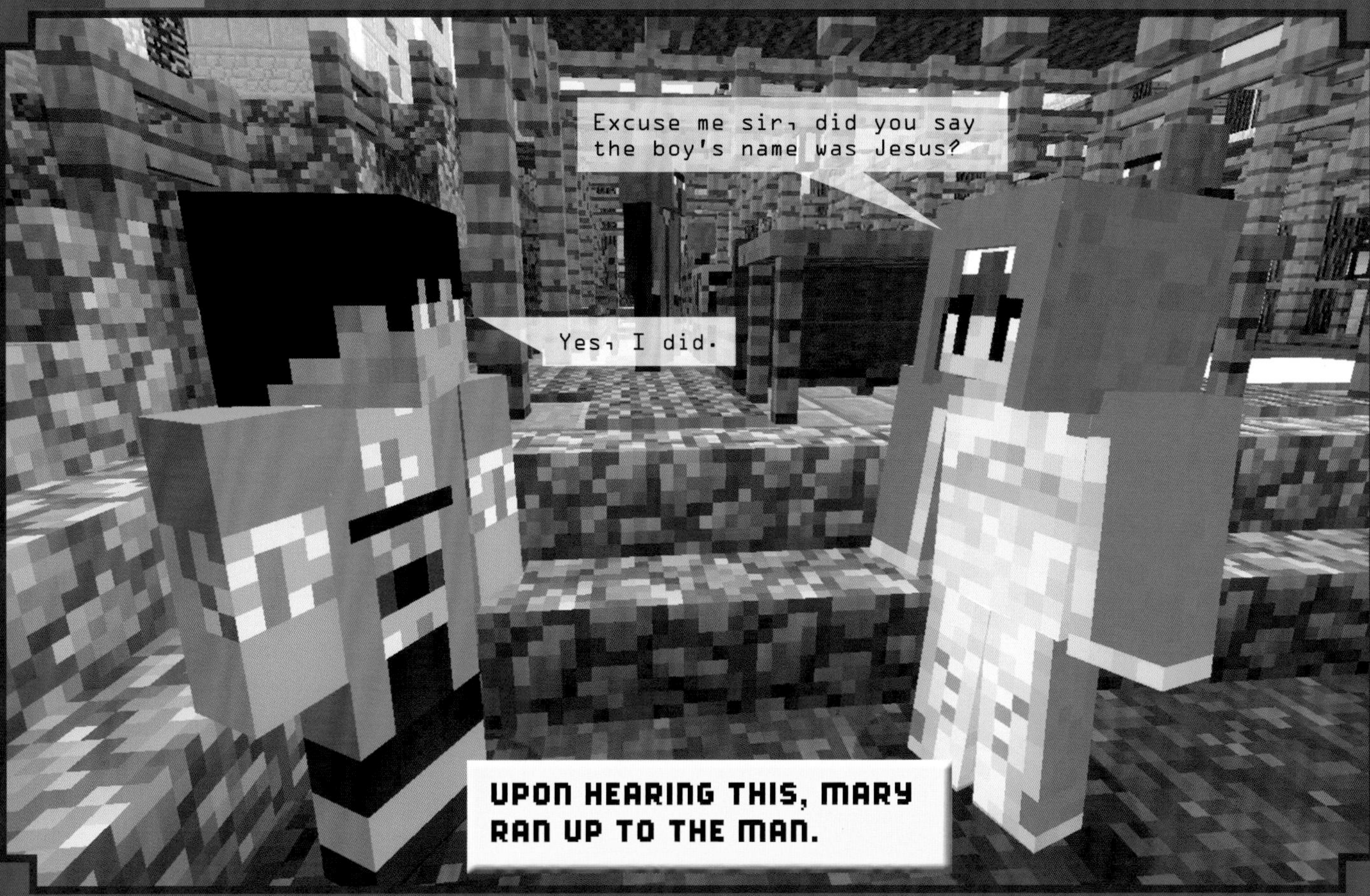
Excuse me sir, did you say the boy's name was Jesus?
Yes, I did.
UPON HEARING THIS, MARY RAN UP TO THE MAN.

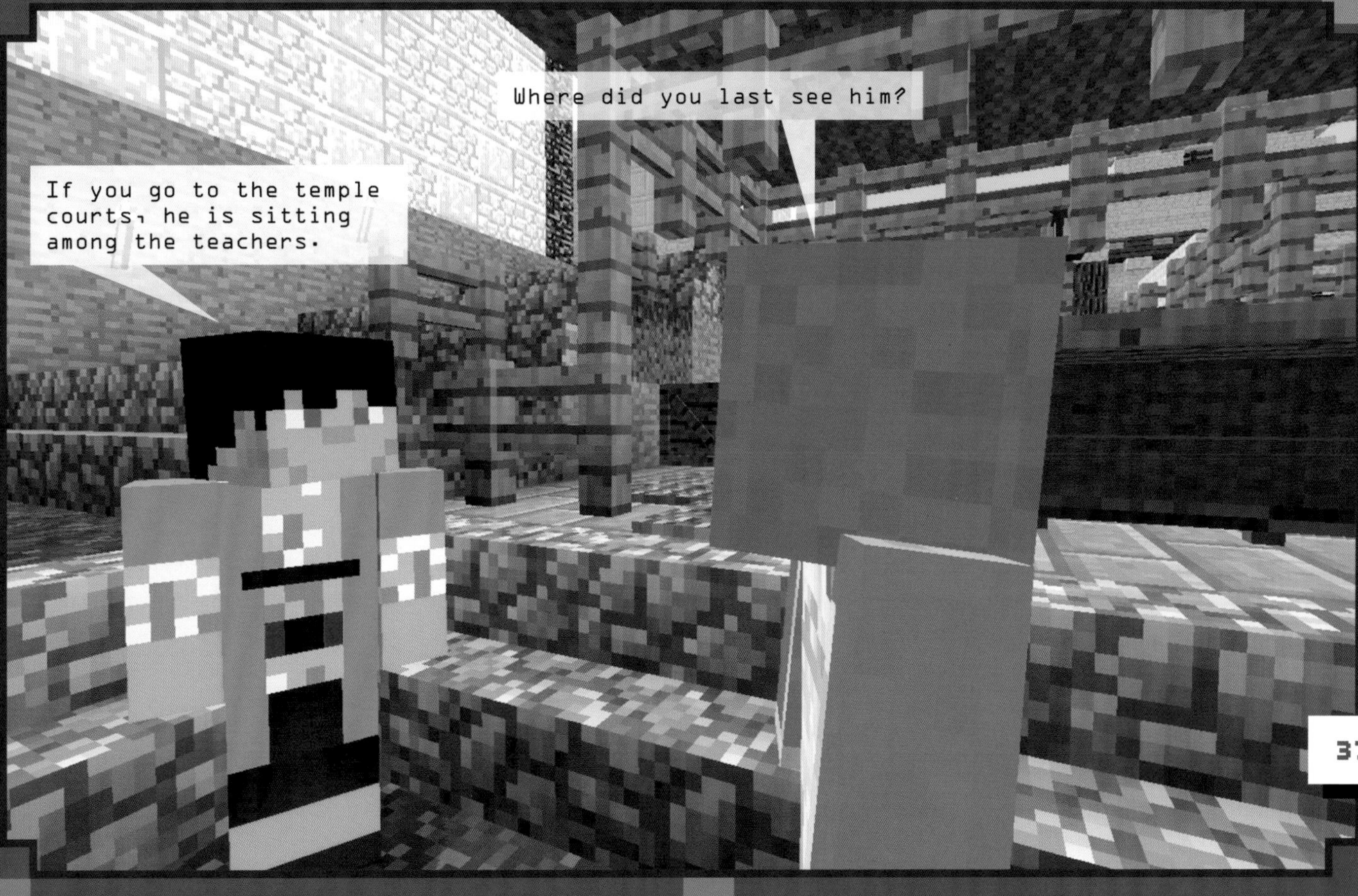
Where did you last see him?
If you go to the temple courts, he is sitting among the teachers.

JOSEPH AND MARY HURRIED TO THE TEMPLE COURTS.

What's going on?

All the teachers are learning from Jesus.

WHEN HIS PARENTS SAW JESUS, THEY WERE ASTONISHED.

Son, why have you treated us like this?

MARY RAN UP TO JESUS AND THREW HER ARMS AROUND HER SON.

HIS MOTHER AND FATHER DID NOT UNDERSTAND WHAT JESUS MEANT.

Why were you searching for me? Didn't you know I had to be in my father's house?

Your father and I have been anxiously searching for you.

THEN SHE UNDERSTOOD.

MARY'S HEART SWELLED WITH PRIDE AS SHE WATCHED HER SON CONTINUE HIS TEACHINGS.

THEN JESUS WENT DOWN TO NAZARETH WITH HIS PARENTS AND WAS OBEDIENT TO THEM, BUT HIS MOTHER TREASURED THE MEMORY IN HER HEART.

JESUS GOES ABOUT HIS FATHER'S WORK

Jesus has grown. He is now a man.

Yes, he is a great man in my likeness.

AROUND THE SAME TIME, JOHN THE BAPTIST APPEARED AS A PREACHER IN THE JUDEAN WILDERNESS. HE PREACHED THE MESSAGE, "REPENT! FOR THE KINGDOM OF HEAVEN IS UPON YOU." THIS FULFILLED THE PROPHECY OF ISAIAH WHO SAID, "A VOICE SHALL CRY ALOUD IN THE WILDERNESS."

Repent for the time is now. I will baptize you in water. Make ready your hearts.

John, I am ready to be baptized.

JESUS ARRIVED AT THE JORDAN RIVER AND CAME TO JOHN, WHO WAS BAPTIZING VILLAGERS.

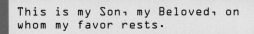

This is my Son, my Beloved, on whom my favor rests.

JESUS ENTERED THE WATER, AND WHEN HE CAME UP, THE SPIRIT OF GOD DESCENDED LIKE A DOVE TO ENLIGHTEN HIM, AND A VOICE FROM HEAVEN WAS HEARD.

If you are the Son of God, tell these stones to become bread so that you may eat and ease your hunger.

Scripture says, "Man does not live by bread alone, but by the word of the living God."

JESUS WAS THEN LED AWAY BY THE SPIRIT INTO THE WILDERNESS. FOR FORTY DAYS AND FORTY NIGHTS HE FASTED, AND AT THE END, THE DEVIL APPEARED. JESUS WAS FAMISHED, AND THE DEVIL TRIED TO LURE HIM.

If you are the Son of God, throw yourself down.

Scripture says, "You are not to put the Lord your God to the test."

THE DEVIL TOOK JESUS TO THE HOLY TEMPLE OF JERUSALEM.

I shall give you all of these kingdoms, if you only will fall down and worship me.

Begone, Satan! Scripture says, "You shall only worship the Lord your God and worship no other."

THE DEVIL THEN TOOK JESUS TO A HIGH MOUNTAIN.

44

The Kingdom of Heaven has come to you this day.

Who is this that speaks with such authority?

Is he a prophet?

He is the wis-est man I have ever heard.

JESUS STOOD BY THE LAKE OF GENNESARET, AND THE PEOPLE LISTENED TO THE WORD OF GOD. HE GOT INTO A BOAT BELONGING TO PETER. THE BOAT PULLED FROM SHORE, THEN JESUS SAT DOWN AND TAUGHT THE PEOPLE FROM THE BOAT.

What an amazing teacher. How does he come by such wisdom?

Let's go far out into the water with the net so we can catch fish.

We have not caught anything, but I will trust in your word.

WHEN HE FINISHED SPEAKING, JESUS TURNED TO THE FISHERMAN, PETER.

JESUS HELPED PETER CAST OUT HIS NETS, AND THEY BECAME FILLED WITH FISH. THE NETS BEGAN TO BREAK. BOTH BOATS WERE SO FULL THAT THEY BEGAN TO SINK.

IT TOOK SOME TIME FOR THE BOATS TO MAKE IT BACK TO SHORE. PETER FELL AT JESUS' KNEES, FOR HE AND ALL HIS COMPANIONS WERE ASTONISHED.

PETER, JAMES, AND JOHN PULLED THEIR BOATS AND FOLLOWED JESUS TO BECOME "FISHERS OF MEN."

JESUS TURNS WATER INTO WINE

Isn't this where Jesus begins
to do miracles?

SOON, JESUS HAD RETURNED TO GALILEE.

Good sir! My master invites you to join us at his wedding. Will you bless us with your presence?

I would love to come and celebrate the union.

ON THE THIRD DAY AFTER HIS ARRIVAL, A WEDDING WAS HELD WHICH JESUS' FAMILY WAS INVITED TO.

Son, there is a problem. Can you help with the wine?

Why? I would prefer not to be involved, but I will do what you ask.

WHEN THE WINE WAS GONE, JESUS' MOTHER CAME TO HIM.

Do as my son says.

Yes, ma'am.

MARY WENT TO THE MASTER'S SERVANT.

51

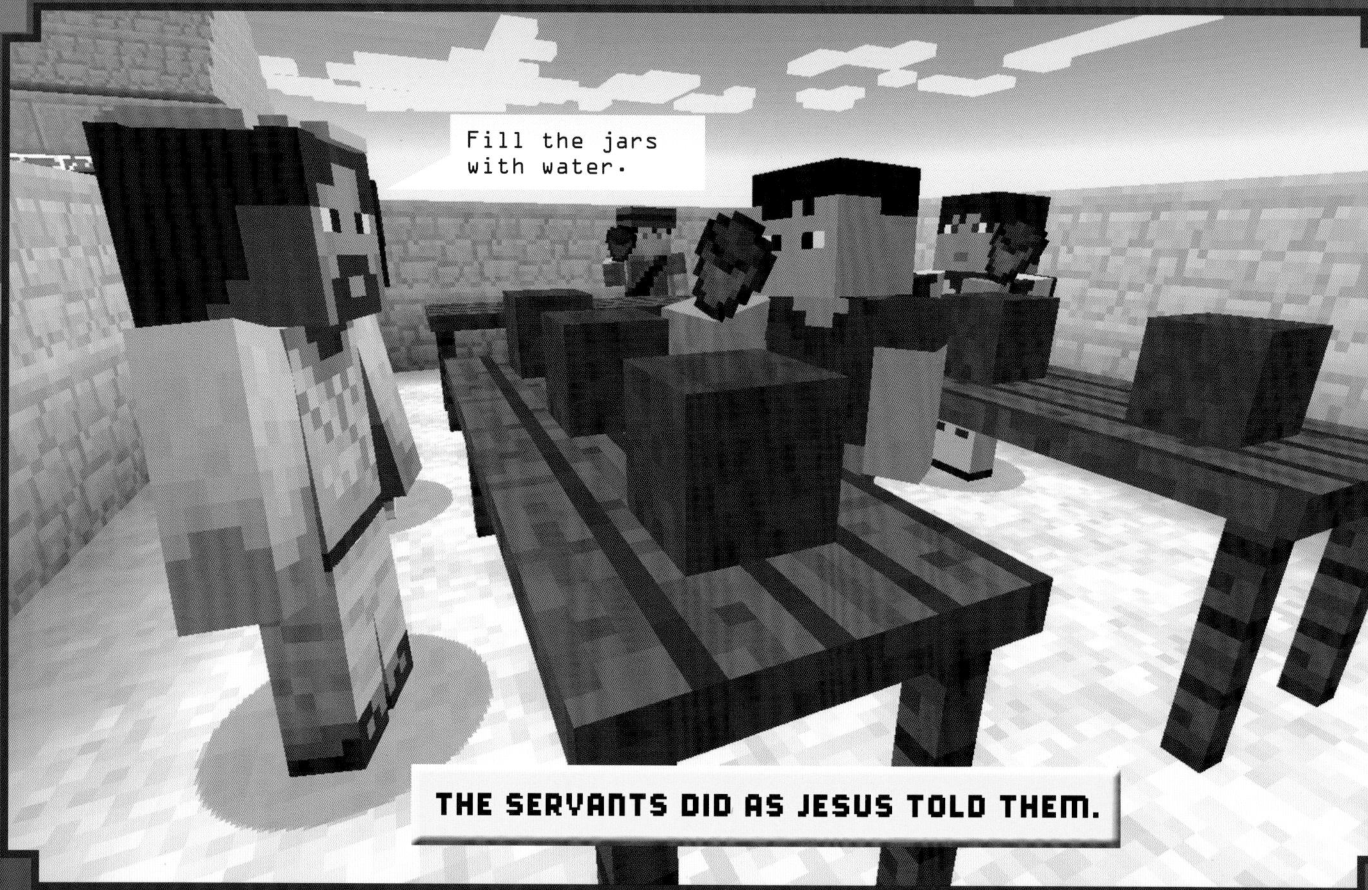
Fill the jars with water.
THE SERVANTS DID AS JESUS TOLD THEM.

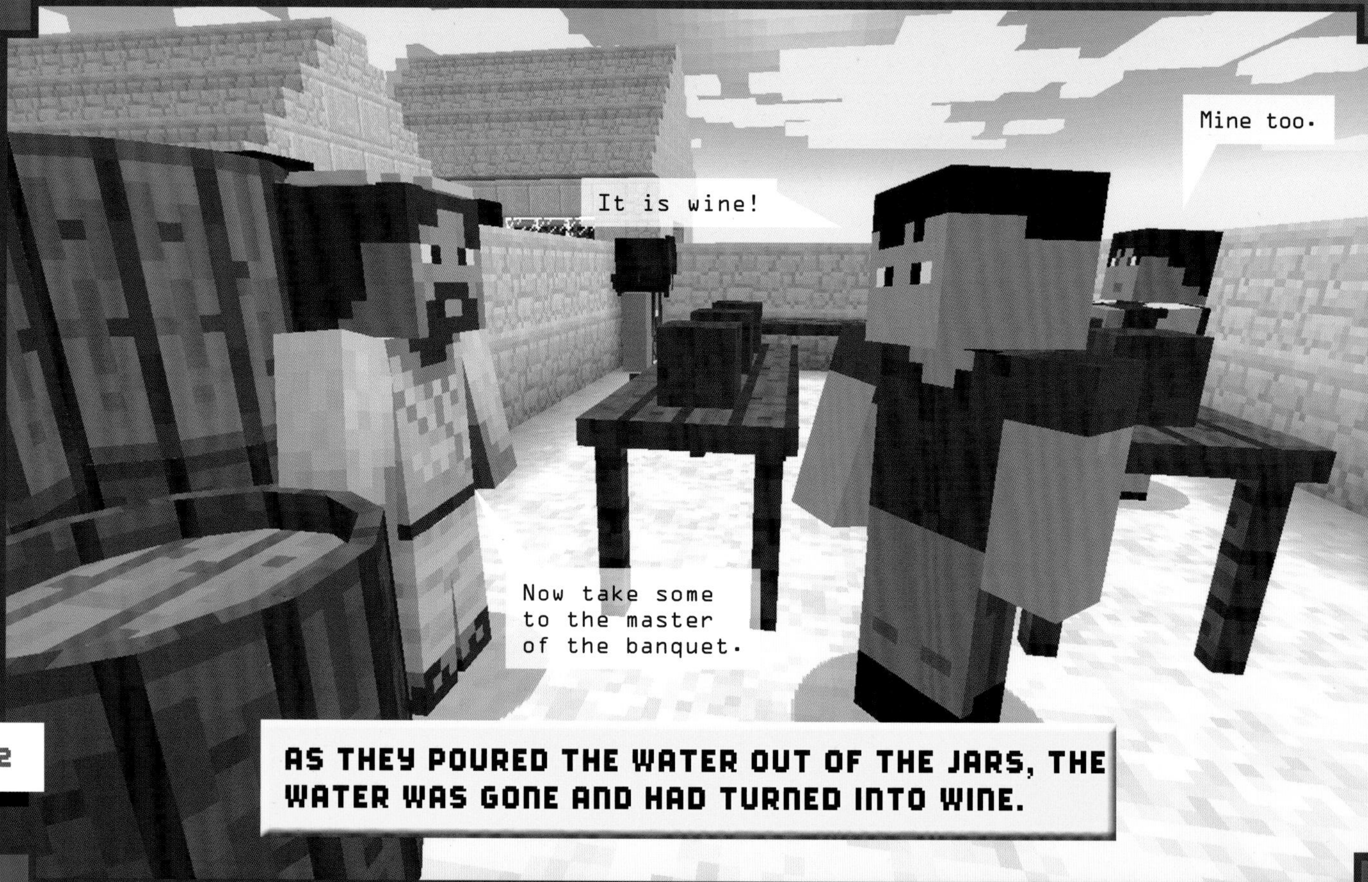
It is wine!
Mine too.
Now take some to the master of the banquet.
AS THEY POURED THE WATER OUT OF THE JARS, THE WATER WAS GONE AND HAD TURNED INTO WINE.

THE MASTER OF THE BANQUET DRANK THE WINE.

The wine had run out and Jesus, the son of Joseph, turned water into wine.

This is the best wine I have tasted. Did I not order the best wine to be served first, and now you serve it last?

THE GUESTS OF THE WEDDING WERE LEFT TO WONDER AT THIS MIRACLE. THIS WAS THE FIRST SIGN THAT REVEALED THE GLORY TO COME.

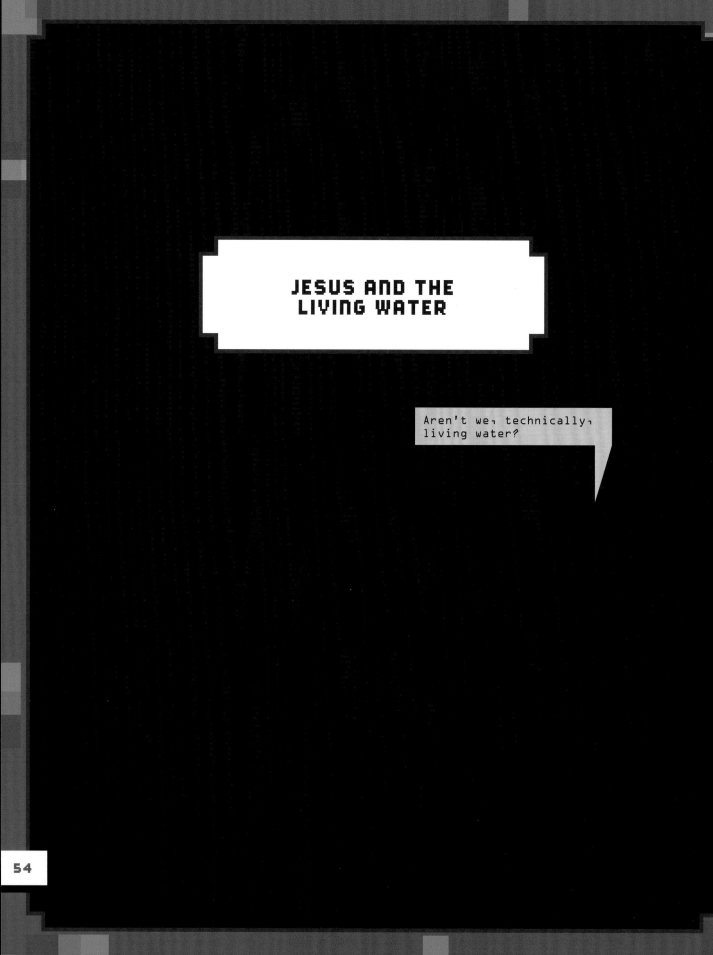

JESUS AND THE
LIVING WATER

Aren't we, technically, living water?

AFTER TRAVELING TO JUDEA TO TEACH FOR A WHILE, JESUS HEADED BACK DOWN THE ROAD TO RETURN TO GALILEE.

ON HIS ROUTE, HE CAME TO A TOWN IN SAMARIA CALLED SYCHAR, WHICH IS WHERE JACOB'S WELL WAS LOCATED. JESUS, TIRED AS HE WAS FROM THE JOURNEY, SAT DOWN BY THE WELL, BUT HAD NOTHING TO DRAW WATER WITH TO QUENCH HIS THIRST.

55

A SAMARITAN WOMAN MARCHED UP THE ROAD TOWARDS JESUS AND THE WELL TO RETRIEVE THE WATER SHE NEEDED, HER TRUSTY BUCKET IN HAND.

JESUS FELT RELIEVED TO SEE HER.

Will you give me a drink?

But you are a Jew and I am a Samaritan woman. How can you ask me for a drink?

THE WOMAN WAS SURPRISED THAT JESUS WOULD ASSOCIATE WITH HER.

If you knew the gift of God and who it is that asks you for a drink, you would have asked him and he would have given you living water.

JESUS ANSWERED HER.

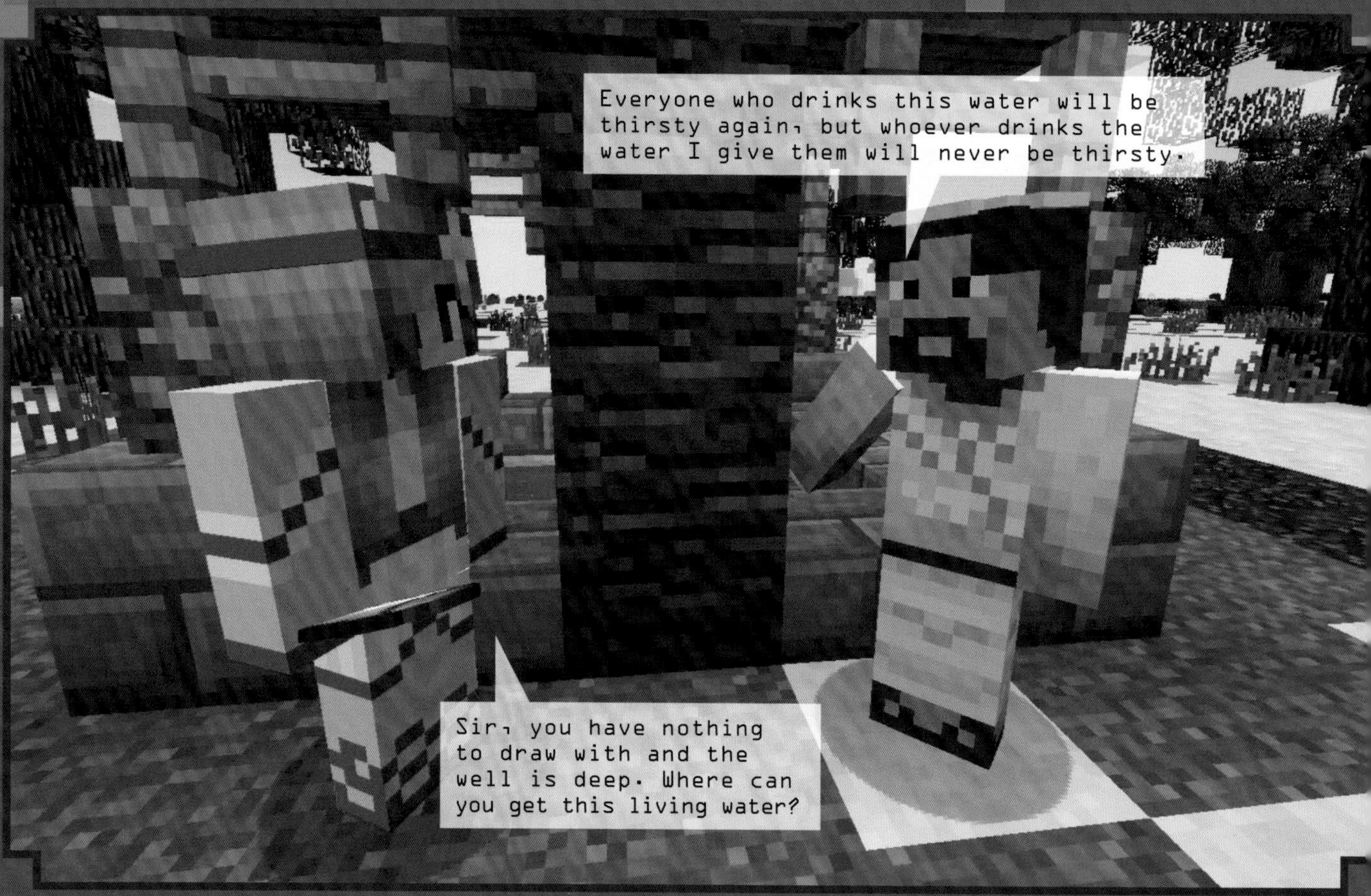
Everyone who drinks this water will be thirsty again, but whoever drinks the water I give them will never be thirsty.
Sir, you have nothing to draw with and the well is deep. Where can you get this living water?

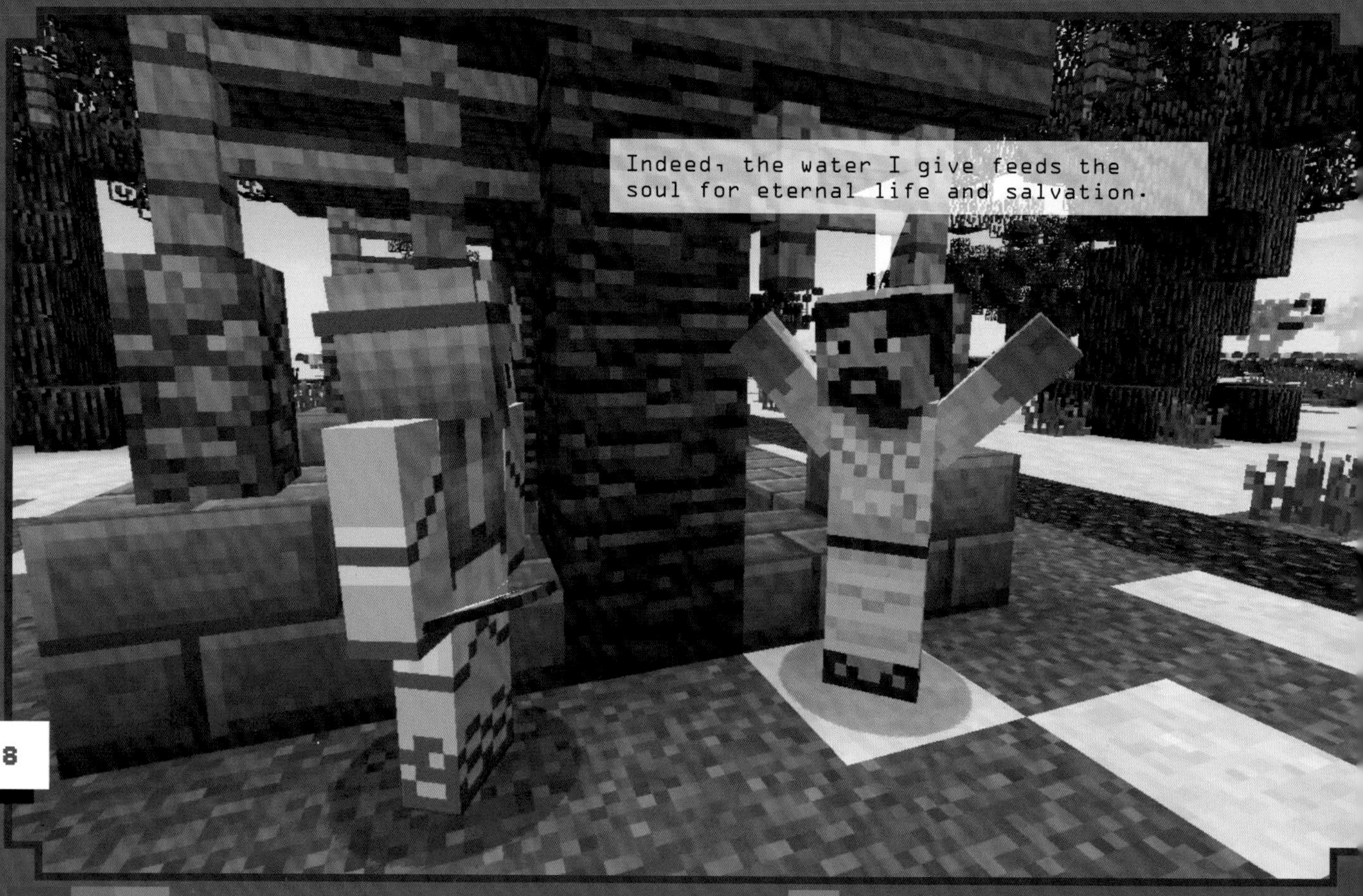
Indeed, the water I give feeds the soul for eternal life and salvation.

I get the sense you are a prophet. Our ancestors worshipped on this mountain, but you Jews claim that the place where we must worship is in Jerusalem.

A time is coming when you will worship the Father, neither on this mountain nor in Jerusalem. A time is coming when the true worshippers will worship the Father in the Spirit and in truth, for they are the kind of worshippers the Father seeks.

I know that the Messiah, called Christ, is coming and will explain everything to us. Do you know him?

Of course I know him. He is me!

THE WOMAN FELL FACE-DOWN IN FRONT OF JESUS.

My Lord!

Rise, my child, for your faith has made you born again, and you have the living spring within you.

JESUS HEALS THE SICK

Wow, it didn't take long for Jesus to develop a following.

For everyone who asks, receives. Everyone who seeks, finds. And to everyone who knocks, the door will be opened.

PEOPLE GATHERED IN THE VILLAGE OF GALILEE TO HEAR JESUS SPEAK.

A GROUP CARRIED A PARA-LYZED MAN ON A MAT TO LAY HIM BEFORE JESUS.

WHEN THEY COULD NOT FIND A WAY THROUGH THE CROWD, THEY WENT UP ON THE ROOF AND LOW-ERED HIM ON HIS MAT THROUGH THE ROOF.

Friend, your sins are forgiven.

Please, heal me so I may walk again.

THE CROWD OF PEOPLE GREW SILENT AND WAITED TO HEAR WHAT JESUS WOULD SAY. JESUS LAID HIS HAND ON THE PARALYZED MAN.

He is no longer just teaching, he is now forgiving sins.

THE PHARISEES AND THE TEACHERS OF THE LAW GATHERED.

Why are you thinking these things? I want you to know that the Son of Man has authority on Earth to forgive sins.

JESUS KNEW WHAT THEY WERE THINKING.

Get up, take your mat, and go home.

HE THEN SPOKE TO THE PARALYZED MAN.

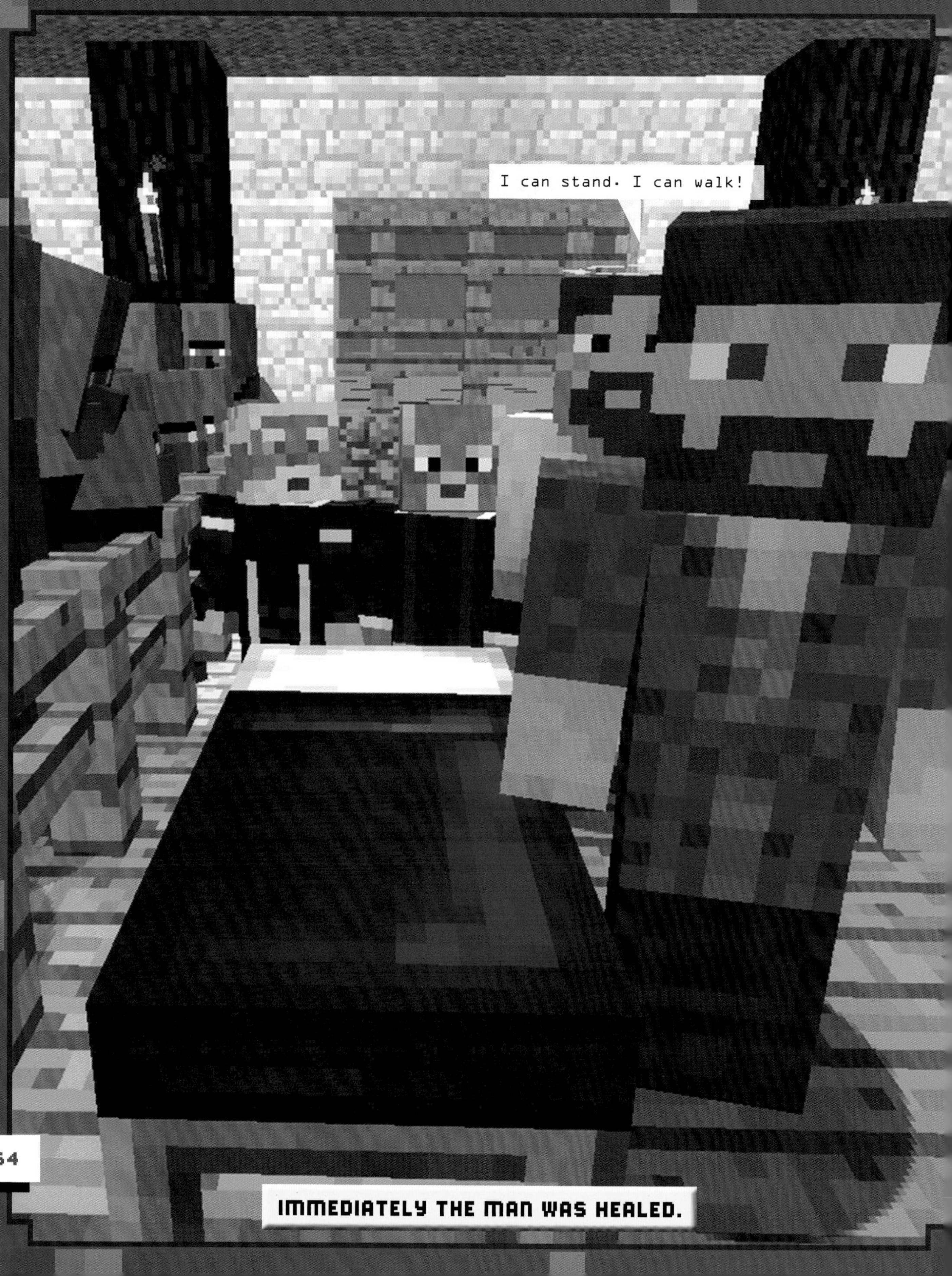
I can stand. I can walk!
IMMEDIATELY THE MAN WAS HEALED.

This was a lovely meal. I thank you for your kindness.

Could we hear more of your interpretation of the Laws?

THEN ONE OF THE PHARISEES INVITED JESUS TO HAVE DINNER AT HIS HOUSE.

Forgive me of my sins.

A SINFUL WOMAN LEARNED THAT JESUS WAS AT THE PHARISEE'S HOUSE, SO SHE CAME THERE WITH AN ALABASTER JAR OF PERFUME. AS SHE STOOPED AT HIS FEET WEEPING, SHE WET HIS FEET WITH HER TEARS. SHE WIPED HER TEARS WITH HER HAIR, KISSED HIS FEET, AND POURED PERFUME ON THEM.

If this man were a prophet, he would know what kind of woman she is.

Two people owed money to a certain moneylender. One owed him five hundred denarii, and the other fifty. Neither of them had the money to pay him back, so he forgave the debts of both. Now which of them will love him more?

JESUS CALLED THE PHARISEES OVER TO ASK THEM A QUESTION.

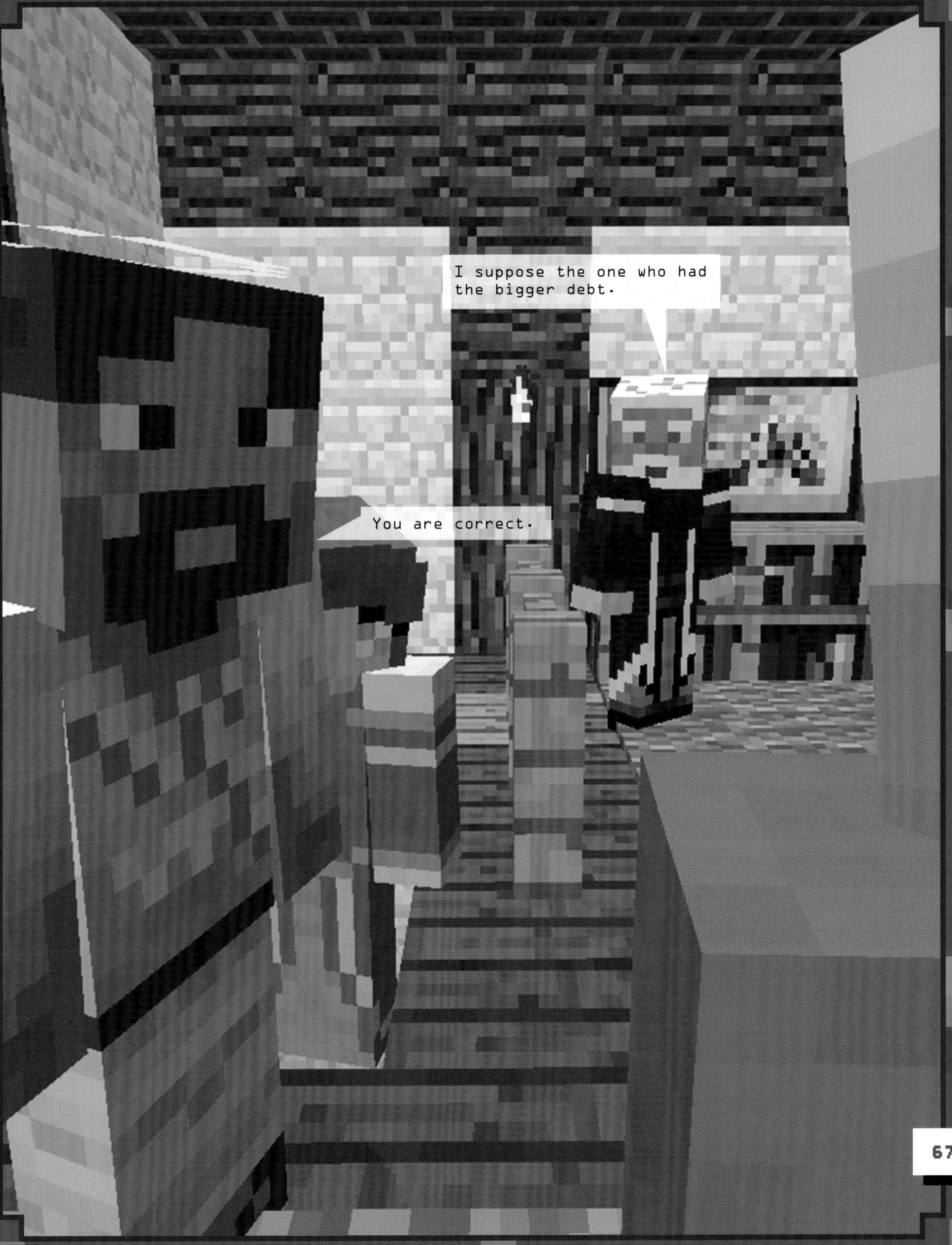
I suppose the one who had the bigger debt.
You are correct.

I came into your house. You did not give me any water for my feet, but she wet my feet with her tears and wiped them with her hair.

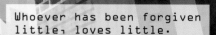

Whoever has been forgiven little, loves little.

I say to you, my child, your sins are forgiven. Go and start your life anew.

He forgave
her sins?

THE PHARISEES BEGAN TO TALK AMONG THEMSELVES.

Your faith has saved
you. Go now, in peace.

Thank you, my Lord.
I will begin my life
anew as a servant of
the Lord.

Lord, if you are willing, you can make me clean.

Yes, be clean!

WHILE JESUS WAS IN ONE OF THE TOWNS, A MAN CAME ALONG WHO HAD LEPROSY. HE PRAYED, AND BEGGED JESUS FOR HELP. JESUS TOUCHED THE MAN.

I am clean!

THE LEPROSY LEFT THE MAN.

Go, show yourself to the priest, and offer the sacrifices that Moses commanded for your cleansing as a testimony to them.

THEN JESUS ORDERED HIM:

THE NEWS SPREAD, AND MANY PEOPLE CAME TO HEAR JESUS AND TO BE HEALED OF THEIR SICKNESSES.

Please help me!

WHEN JESUS ENTERED CAPERNAUM, A ROMAN SOLDIER ASKED HIM TO HEAL HIS SICK SON. THE ROMAN SOLDIER LEFT HIM AND RETURNED TO FIND HIS CHILD HEALED.

JESUS WAS MOVED BY THE FAITH OF THE ROMAN PEOPLE.

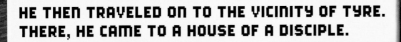

HE THEN TRAVELED ON TO THE VICINITY OF TYRE.
THERE, HE CAME TO A HOUSE OF A DISCIPLE.

JESUS' ARRIVAL IN TYRE HAD BEEN A SECRET, YET WORD
OF HIS PRESENCE COULD NOT BE CONTAINED. PEOPLE CAME
IN DROVES TO HEAR HIS WORDS.

I promise I will find help for you. There is a man people say can heal the sick.

A WOMAN, WHOSE LITTLE DAUGHTER WAS POSSESSED BY AN IMPURE SPIRIT, HEARD THAT JESUS WAS IN HER TOWN.

May I please see the man named Jesus?

I will speak to him. Wait here.

THE WOMAN WENT TO THE HOUSE WHERE JESUS WAS STAYING.

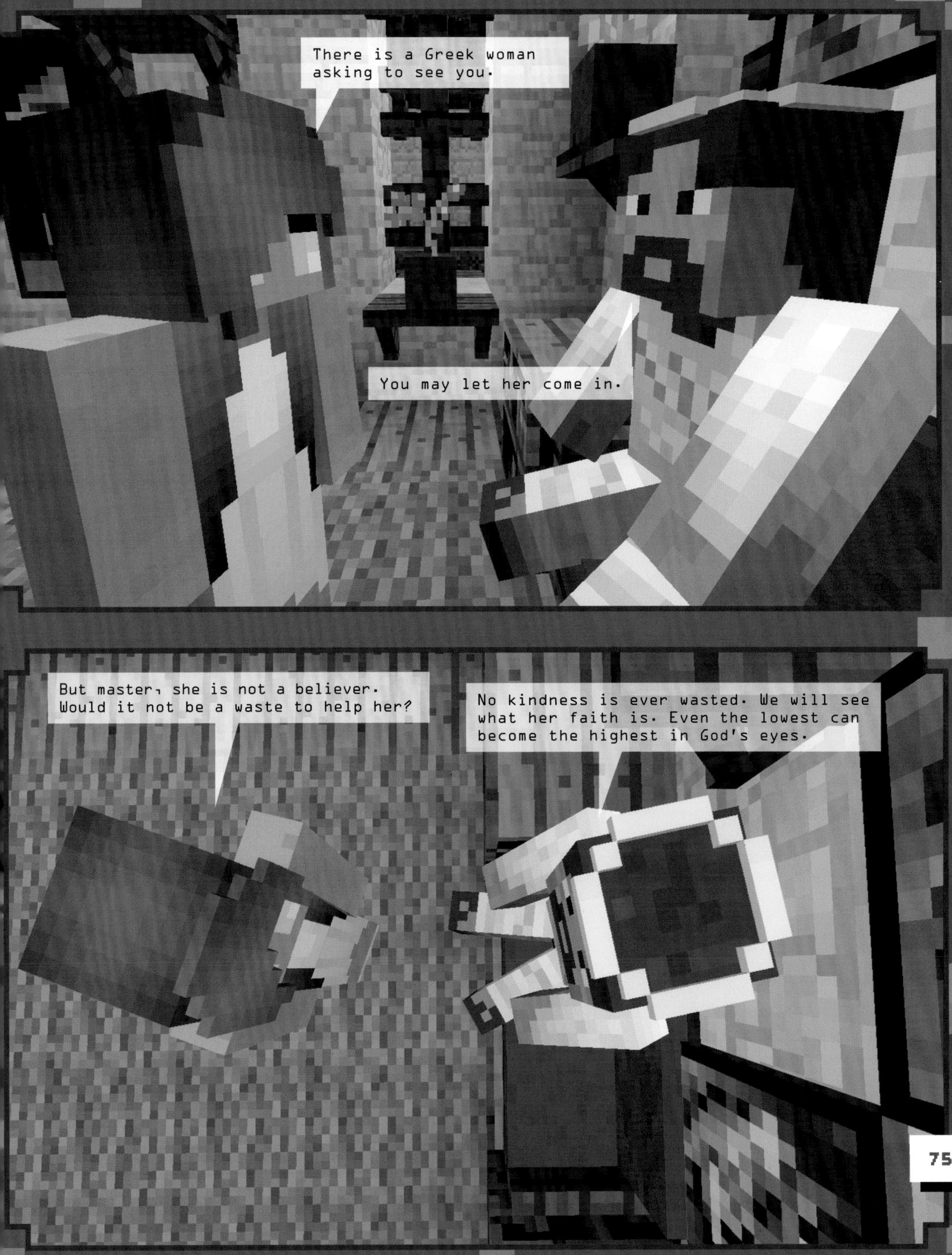

There is a Greek woman asking to see you.
You may let her come in.
But master, she is not a believer. Would it not be a waste to help her?
No kindness is ever wasted. We will see what her faith is. Even the lowest can become the highest in God's eyes.

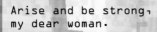

Arise and be strong,
my dear woman.

SHE CAME BEFORE JESUS AND FELL AT HIS FEET.

Please, drive out the
demon that has taken
control of my daughter.

ONCE SHE HAD GATHERED HERSELF, SHE BEGAN TO BEG.

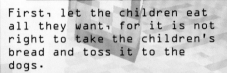

First, let the children eat all they want, for it is not right to take the children's bread and toss it to the dogs.

Even the dogs under the table eat the children's crumbs.

For such a reply, you may go; the demon has left your daughter.

THE WOMAN LEFT JESUS PRAISING HIM.

SHE WENT HOME AND FOUND HER CHILD STANDING BEFORE HER. THE DEMON WAS GONE.

Praise God, for I have seen him do great miracles.

WHEN THE CHILD SAW HER MOTHER, SHE RAN TO HER, AND THE TWO EMBRACED.

SOON AFTER, JESUS LEFT TYRE AND WENT DOWN TO THE SEA OF GALILEE, TO THE TOWN OF DECOPOLIS.

THERE, SOME PEOPLE BROUGHT HIM A MAN WHO WAS DEAF AND COULD NOT TALK.

JESUS TOOK THE MAN ASIDE, AWAY FROM THE CROWD.

JESUS STRETCHED OUT HIS HAND AND TOUCHED THE
MAN'S EARS. THEN HE TOUCHED HIS TONGUE.

81

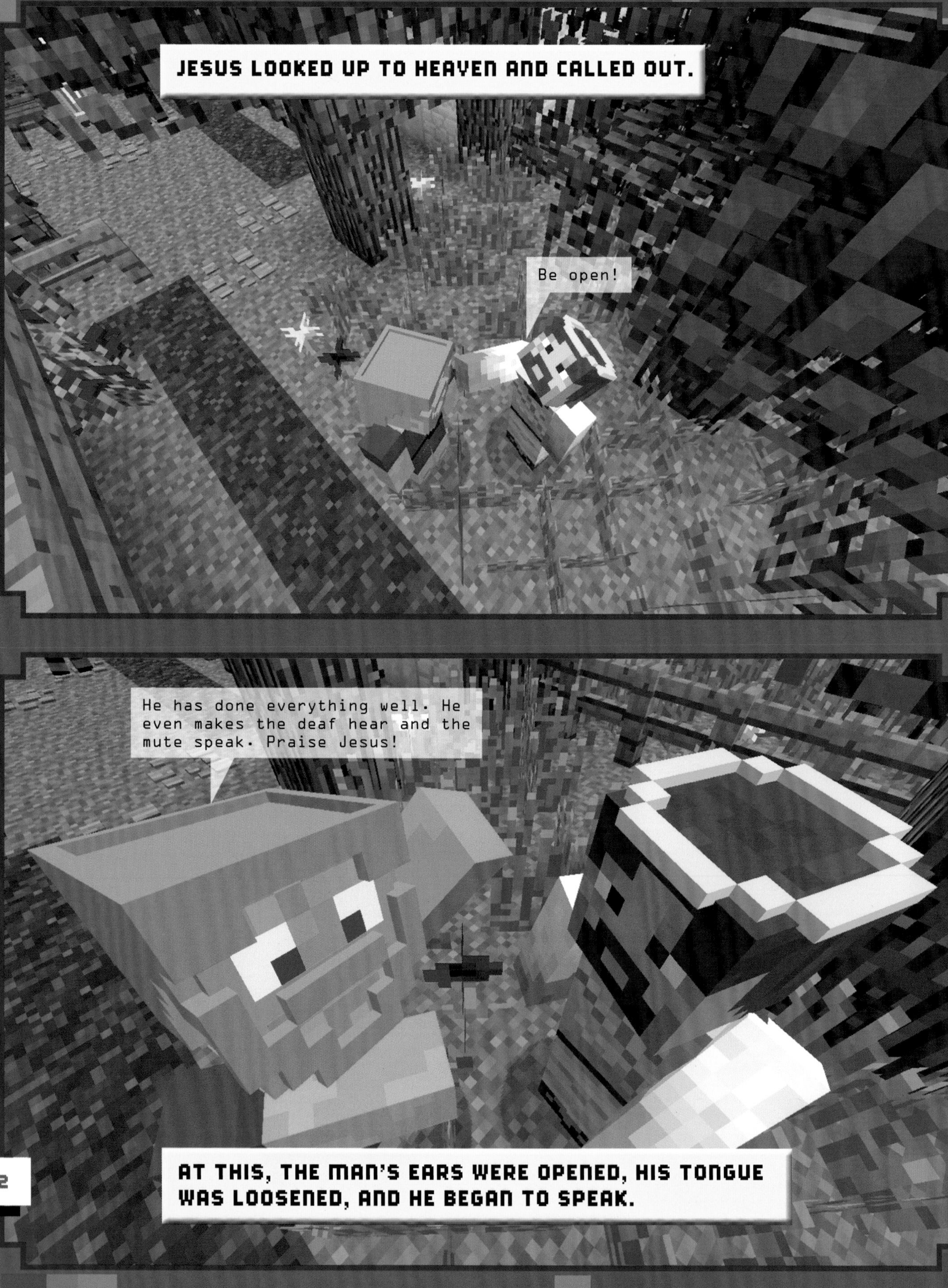
JESUS LOOKED UP TO HEAVEN AND CALLED OUT.
Be open!
He has done everything well. He even makes the deaf hear and the mute speak. Praise Jesus!
AT THIS, THE MAN'S EARS WERE OPENED, HIS TONGUE WAS LOOSENED, AND HE BEGAN TO SPEAK.

THE MAN RETURNED TO THE GATHERED GROUP WITH A RENEWED SENSE OF JOY AND SELF-WORTH.

Jesus is a hero!

It's a miracle!

THE PEOPLE SAW WHAT HAD HAPPENED TO THE MAN AND CALLED OUT, PRAISING JESUS.

Please—I'm trying to keep a low profile.

JESUS COMMANDED THEM NOT TO TELL ANYONE OF THIS MIRACLE.

Jesus makes the deaf hear. He is the Messiah!

Jesus makes the blind see.

Jesus heals!

THE PEOPLE WERE TOO OVERWHELMED WITH AMAZEMENT. THEY TOLD EVERYONE THEY FOUND.

JESUS HEALS ON THE SABBATH

According to Moses' Laws, Jesus shouldn't be healing on the Sabbath . . . has something changed?

SOMETIME LATER, JESUS WENT UP TO JERUSALEM. THERE, NEAR THE SHEEP GATE, WAS A POOL WHICH DISABLED PEOPLE WOULD LIE NEAR.

AN ELDERLY MAN LAY BY THE POOLSIDE BARELY ABLE TO MOVE, HAVING BEEN AN INVALID FOR THIRTY-EIGHT YEARS.

Do you want to get well?

Sir, I have no one to help me into the pool. While I am trying to get in, someone else goes down ahead of me.

Get up! Pick up your mat and walk. You do not need the water to be well. I forgive you of your sins.

JESUS, HAVING PITY ON THE MAN, REACHED OUT TO HIM.

AT ONCE, THE MAN WAS CURED—HE PICKED UP HIS MAT AND WALKED OFF, PRAISING THE LORD.

LATER, JESUS FOUND THE MAN NEAR THE TEMPLE SPEWING HATEFUL WORDS.

See? You are well again! Stop sinning or something worse may happen to you.

That man they call Jesus broke our laws.

Did he now?

THE MAN DID NOT HEED JESUS' WARNING, BUT INSTEAD WENT AWAY AND TOLD THE JEWISH LEADERS THAT HE HAD BEEN HEALED BY JESUS DURING THE SABBATH.

THE LEADERS CAME TO JESUS AND PERSECUTED HIM.

My father is always at His work to this very day, and I, too, am working!

Do you not follow the laws of Moses?

JESUS QUICKLY TOOK HIS LEAVE TO WALK ALONE BESIDE THE LAKE. AS HE MADE HIS WAY ALONG, HE SAW LEVI, SON OF ALPHAEUS, SITTING AT THE TAX COLLECTOR'S BOOTH.

Follow me.

LEVI GOT UP AND WENT WITH JESUS.

WHILE JESUS WAS HAVING DINNER AT LEVI'S HOUSE, MANY TAX COLLECTORS AND SINNERS WERE EATING WITH HIM.

WHEN THE TEACHERS OF THE LAW SAW JESUS EATING WITH THESE LOWLY MISCREANTS, THEY QUESTIONED THE DISCIPLES.

It is not the healthy who need a doctor, but the sick. I have not come to call upon the righteous, but rather the sinners, as they need to connect with God the most.

JESUS OVERHEARD THE PHARISEES AND TURNED TO RESPOND.

DURING THIS TIME, JOHN THE BAPTIST AND HIS DISCIPLES WERE FASTING. SOME AT THE TABLE QUESTIONED JESUS.

How is it that John's disciples are fasting, but yours and you do not?

How can the guests of the bridegroom fast while he is with them?

But the time will come when the bridegroom will be taken from them, and on that day they will fast.

ONE SABBATH, JESUS WAS GOING THROUGH A GRAIN FIELD. AS HIS DISCIPLES WALKED ALONG, THEY BEGAN TO EAT THE GRAIN.

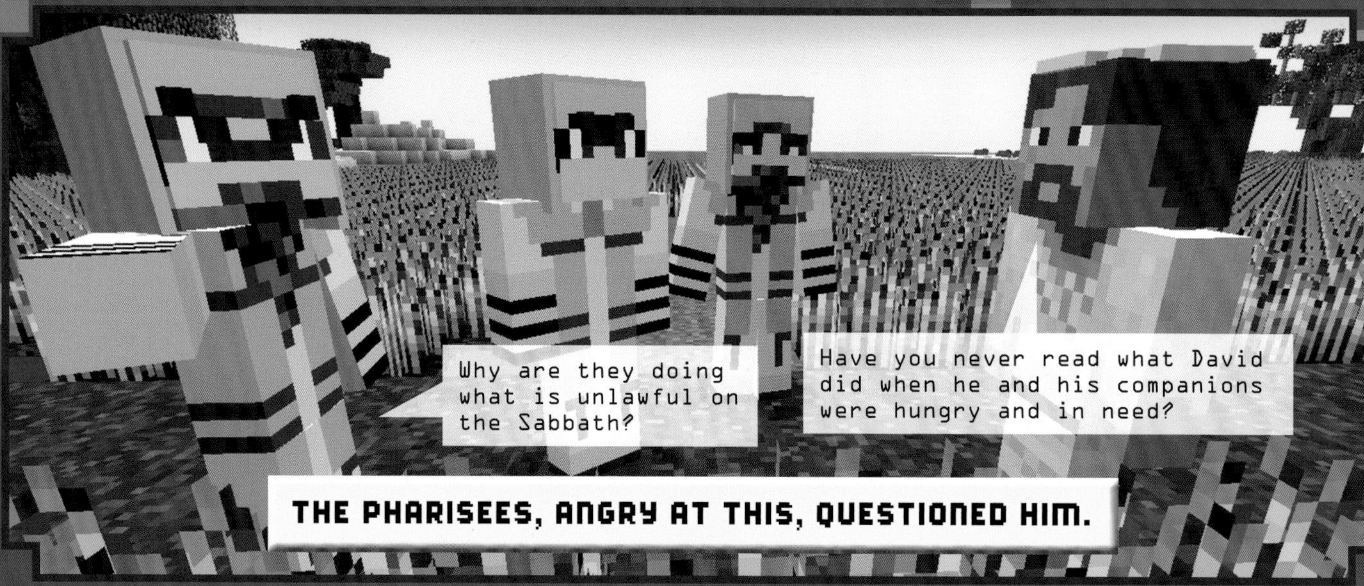
Why are they doing what is unlawful on the Sabbath?
Have you never read what David did when he and his companions were hungry and in need?
THE PHARISEES, ANGRY AT THIS, QUESTIONED HIM.

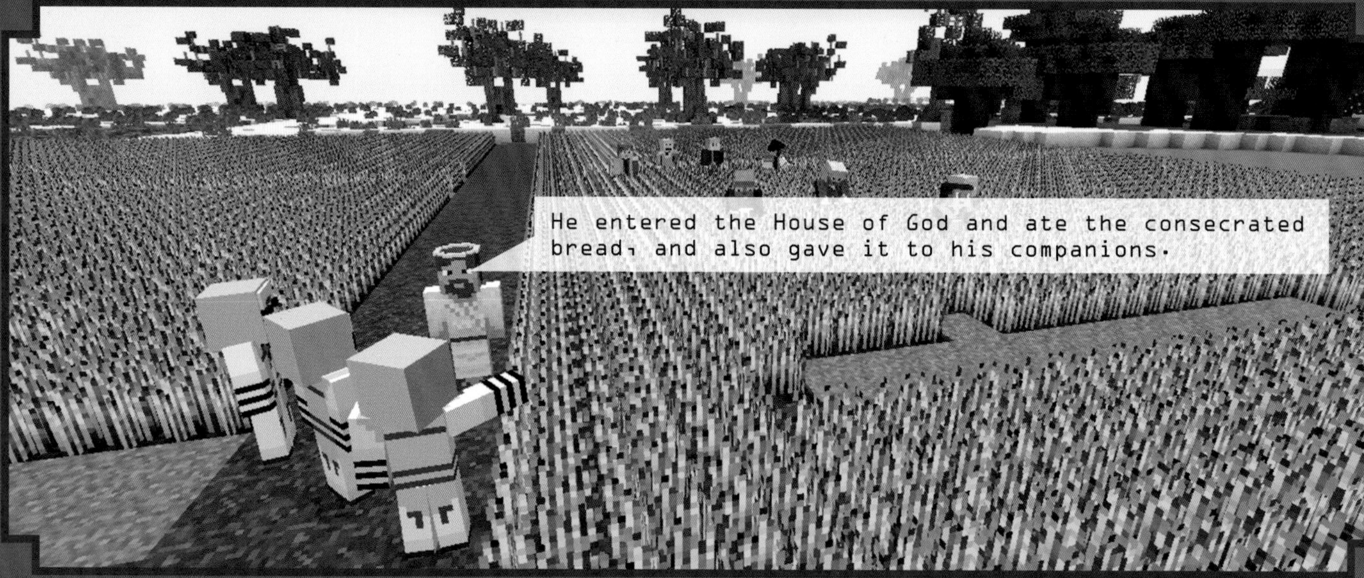
He entered the House of God and ate the consecrated bread, and also gave it to his companions.

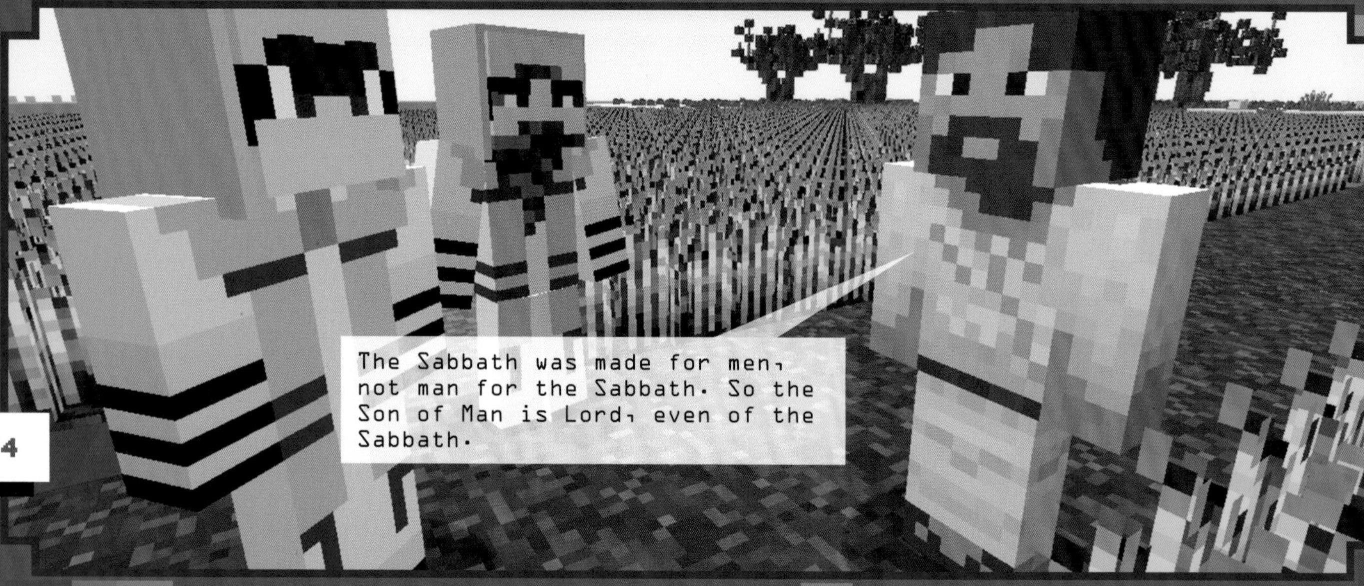
The Sabbath was made for men, not man for the Sabbath. So the Son of Man is Lord, even of the Sabbath.

He claims the laws of God as his own.

How dare he!

He says he is the Lord of the Sabbath.

THE PHARISEES BECAME ANGRY WITH JESUS BECAUSE HE KEPT DOING THINGS ON THE SABBATH.

WHILE THE PHARISEES WERE TALKING, JESUS WENT INTO THE SYNAGOGUE AND BEGAN TO SPEAK TO THOSE GATHERED.

WHILE JESUS PREACHED, A MAN WITH A SHRIVELED HAND CAME UP.

Look! A man with a shriveled hand. Let's see if Jesus will heal on the Sabbath.

If he does, we can accuse him of breaking the laws of Moses.

THE PHARISEES WERE ALWAYS LOOKING FOR A REASON TO ACCUSE JESUS.

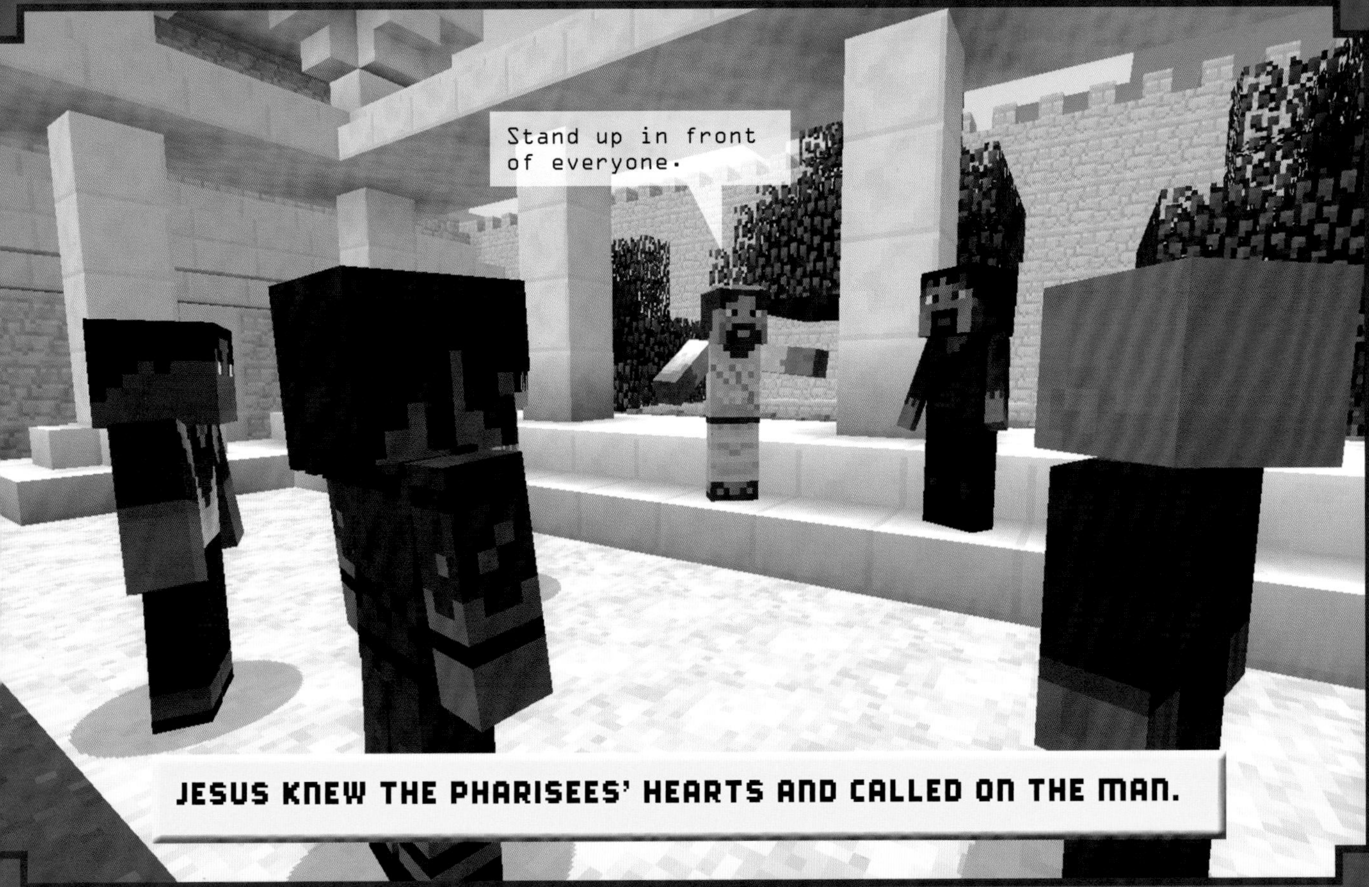
Stand up in front of everyone.
JESUS KNEW THE PHARISEES' HEARTS AND CALLED ON THE MAN.

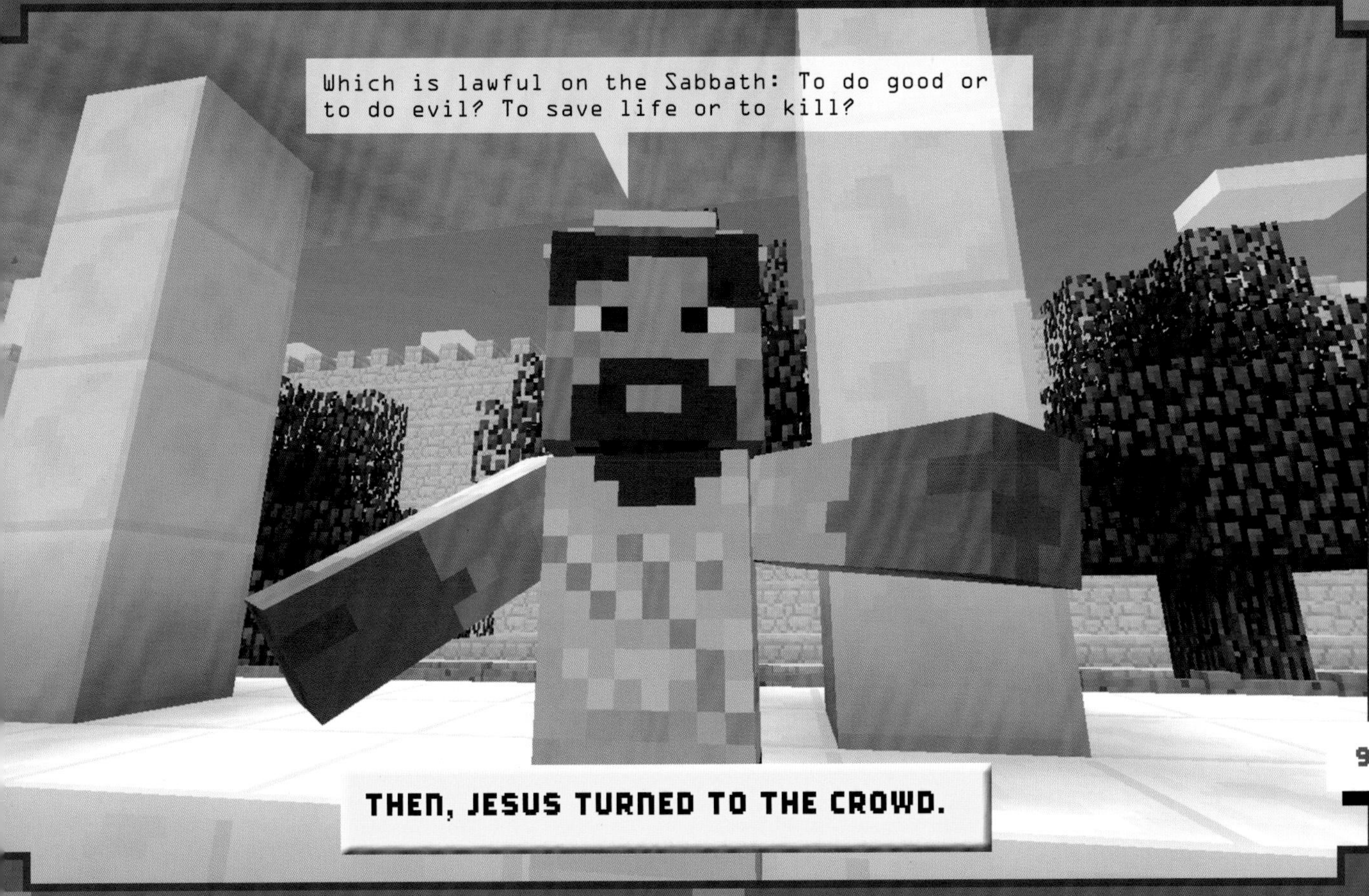
Which is lawful on the Sabbath: To do good or to do evil? To save life or to kill?
THEN, JESUS TURNED TO THE CROWD.

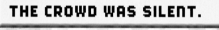

THE CROWD WAS SILENT.

JESUS LOOKED AT THEM WITH SADNESS, FOR THE PHARISEES' HEARTS WERE STUBBORN AND FILLED WITH HATRED. BUT JESUS SPOKE TO THE CRIPPLED MAN ANYWAY.

Stretch out your hand so that all may see what I do in the name of love.

THE MAN STRETCHED OUT HIS HAND TO THE CROWD, AND IT WAS HEALED COMPLETELY.

That is it! We must stop him!

We must go to Jerusalem and speak to the High Priest.

THE PHARISEES, SEEING THIS AND HAVING HEARTS FILLED WITH PRIDE, SET OUT TO PLOT AGAINST JESUS.

SERMON ON THE MOUNT

Is Jesus going to go to Jerusalem?

He still has work to do.

ONE DAY A CROWD FOLLOWED JESUS UP A HILL.

Love your enemies, do good to those who hate you, bless those who curse you, pray for those who mistreat you.

THERE, ON THE HILL, JESUS TAUGHT THEM TO PRAY.

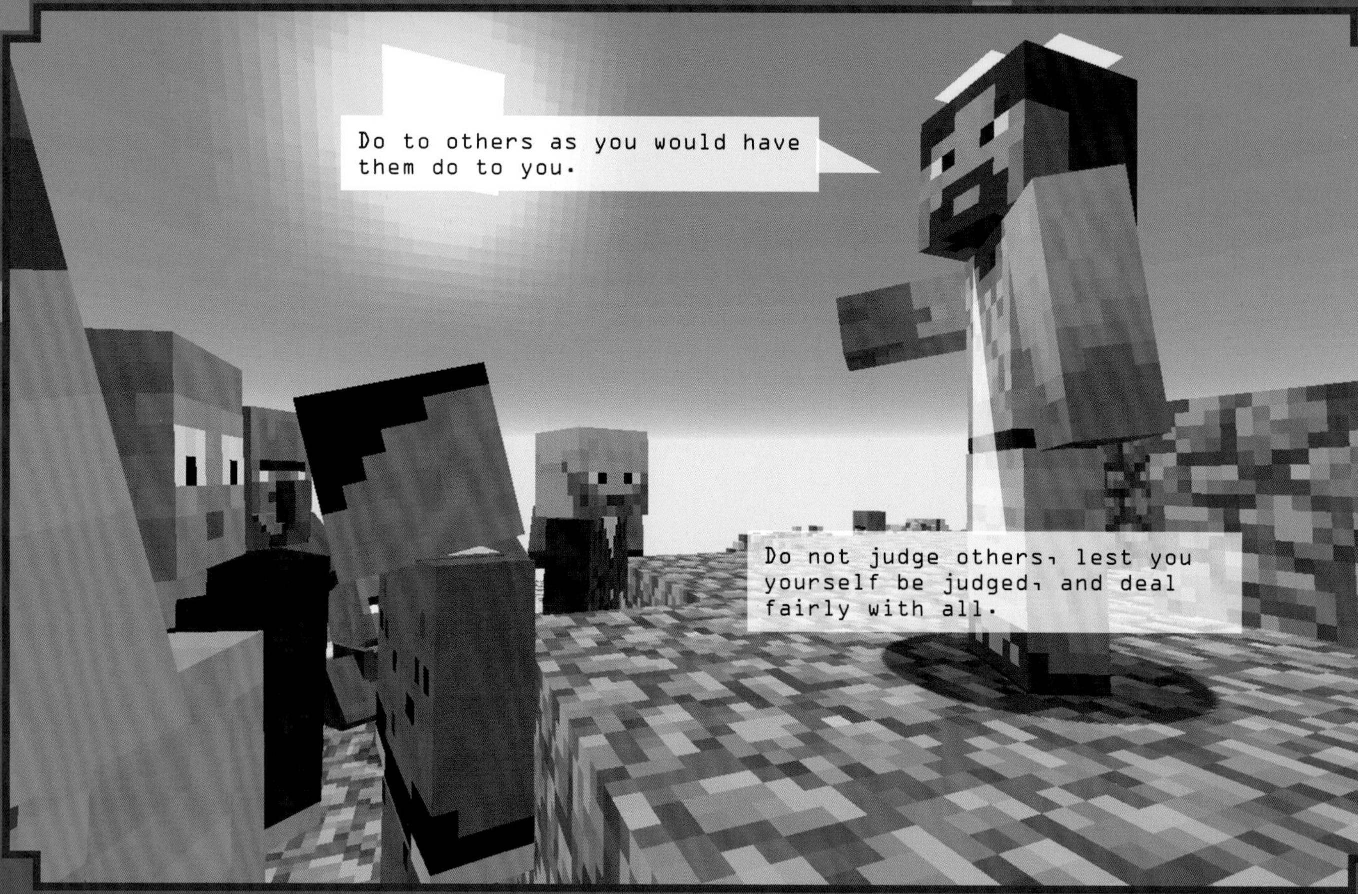
Do to others as you would have them do to you.
Do not judge others, lest you yourself be judged, and deal fairly with all.

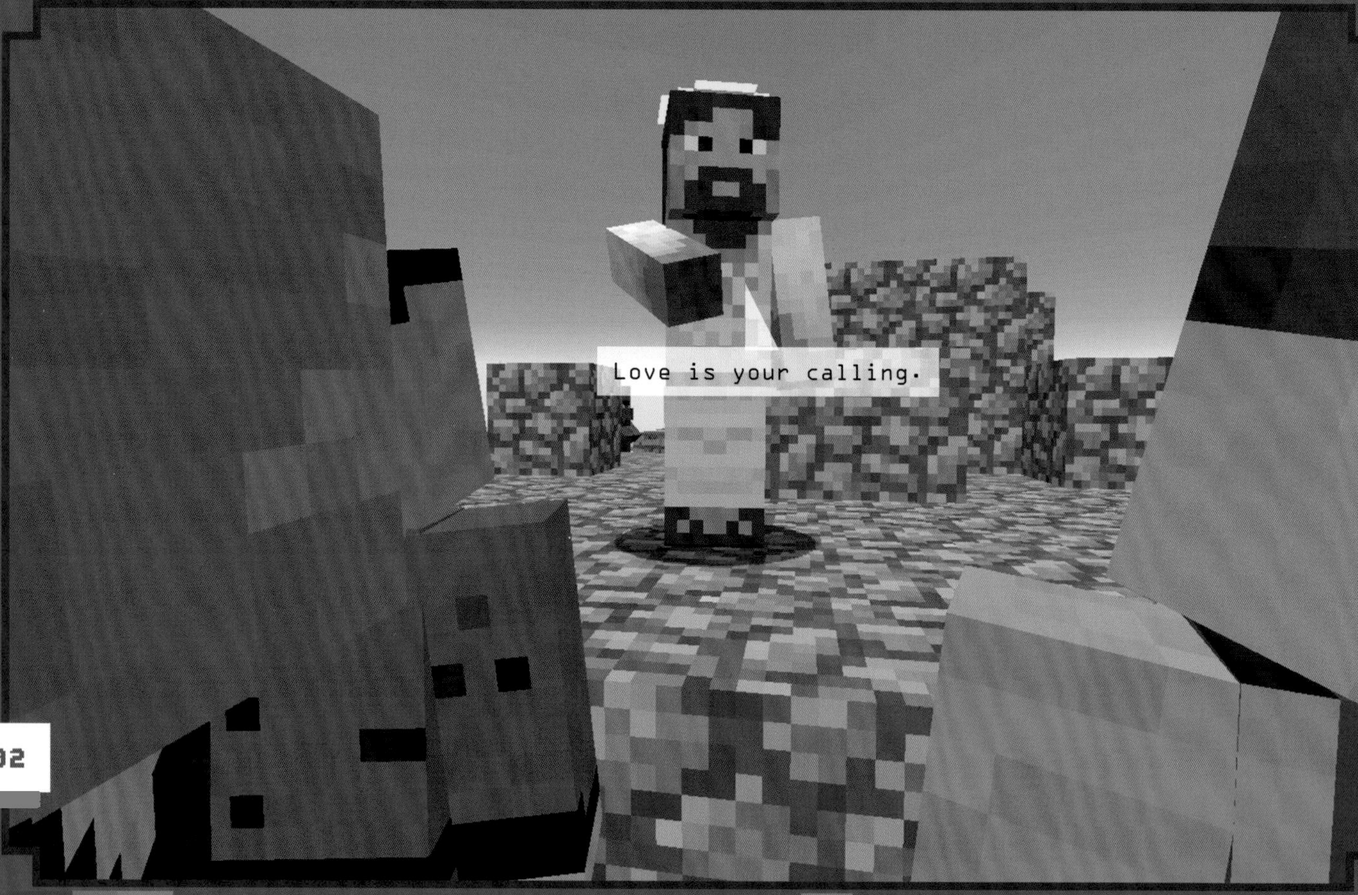
Love is your calling.

JESUS HEADED TO THE LAKE WITH HIS DISCIPLES AND THE CROWD. HE GAVE THE WORD TO CROSS THE LAKE TO THE OTHER SHORE.

JESUS GOT INTO THE BOAT AND HIS DISCIPLES FOLLOWED.

THE BOAT HAD SAILED A GREAT DISTANCE FROM SHORE WHEN ALL AT ONCE, A GREAT STORM AROSE. JESUS WAS EXHAUSTED AND WENT TO TAKE A NAP.

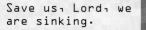

Save us, Lord, we are sinking.

Why are you such cowards? How little faith you have!

THE DISCIPLES WENT TO WAKE JESUS.

Knock it off.

We have seen another miracle.

104

JESUS MADE HIS WAY TO THE SIDE OF THE BOAT. HE REBUKED THE WIND AND WAVES. THERE WAS A DEAD CALM THAT FOLLOWED.

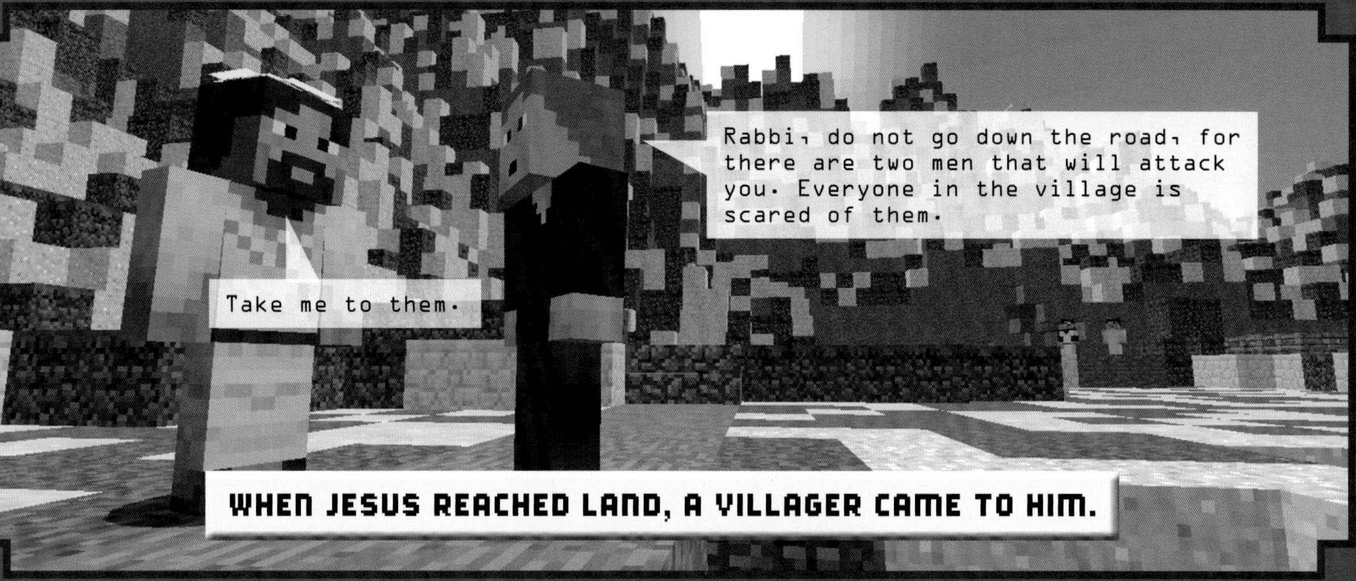
Rabbi, do not go down the road, for there are two men that will attack you. Everyone in the village is scared of them.
Take me to them.
WHEN JESUS REACHED LAND, A VILLAGER CAME TO HIM.

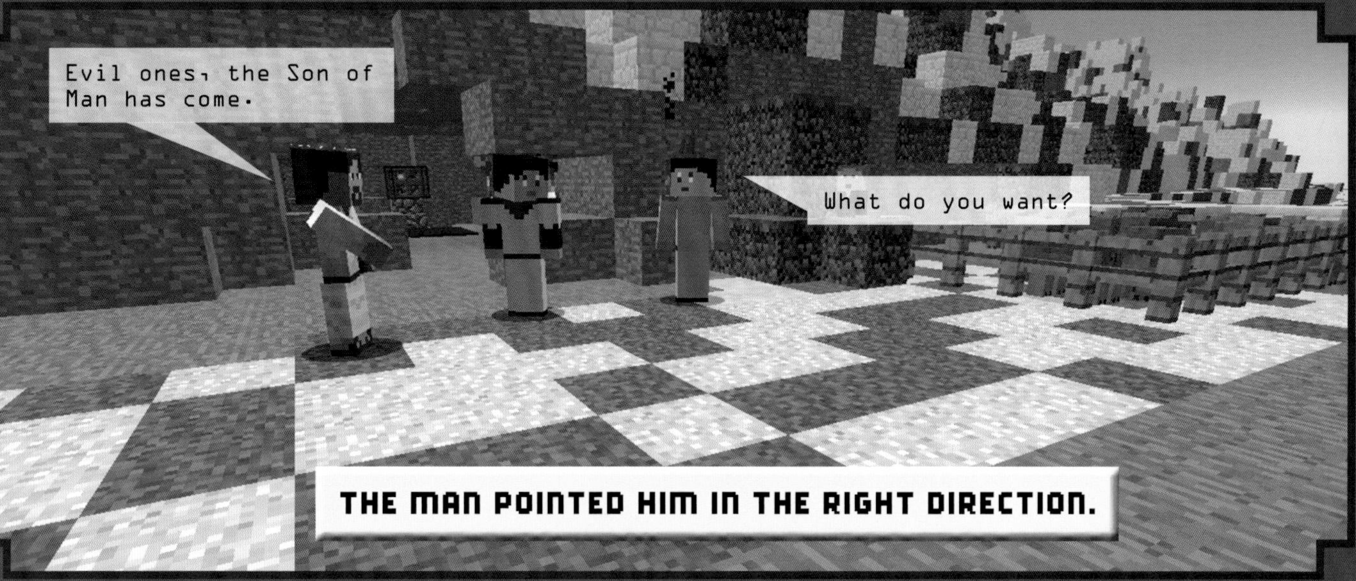
Evil ones, the Son of Man has come.
What do you want?
THE MAN POINTED HIM IN THE RIGHT DIRECTION.

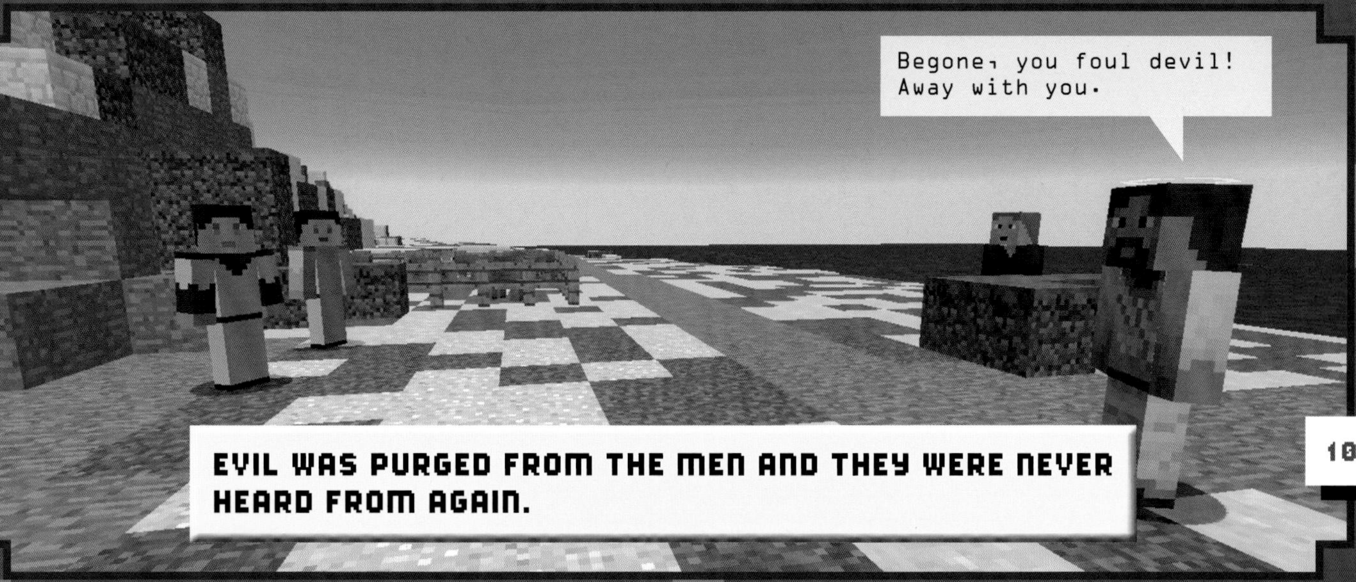
Begone, you foul devil! Away with you.
EVIL WAS PURGED FROM THE MEN AND THEY WERE NEVER HEARD FROM AGAIN.

I am telling you, I saw it with my own eyes! He walked right up to them. They were going to attack, but when they saw him, they stopped. Then he commanded them with one breath and they were gone.

Can it be true?

THE MAN THAT SAW THIS WENT FAR AND WIDE RECOUNTING HOW JESUS HAD CAST OUT THE DEVILS.

Whoever humbles himself like a child is the greatest in the Kingdom of Heaven.

JESUS CONTINUED ON HIS WAY. HE WENT AROUND TO ALL THE VILLAGES TEACHING THE GOOD NEWS.

JESUS GAVE HIS TWELVE DISCIPLES AUTHORITY TO CAST OUT UN-CLEAN SPIRITS AND TO CURE EVERY KIND OF AILMENT AND DISEASE.

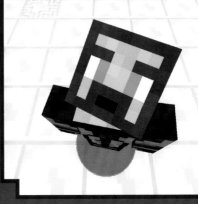

THE CHOSEN FEW TO CONTINUE THE WORK OF JESUS AS HIS APOSTLES WERE JOHN, JAMES, THE SON OF ZEBEDEE, PETER, MATTHEW, BARNABUS, JUDAS, BARTHOLOMEW, JAMES, THE SON OF ALPHAEUS, PHILIP, SIMON A. THOMAS, AND ANDREW.

JESUS' PARABLES

Jesus has a lot of followers now. How will he teach them all?

Jesus teaches through the telling of parables and the asking of questions.

JESUS CAME BY THE LAKESIDE ONCE MORE. THERE WERE MANY PEOPLE GATHERED AROUND HIM.

Let me begin with the story of "The Sower of the Good Seed."

IN ORDER FOR ADULTS AND CHILDREN TO REMEMBER AND UNDERSTAND HIS LESSONS, HE TAUGHT THEM THROUGH THE TELLING OF PARABLES.

PARABLE

A SOWER WENT OUT TO SOW HIS FIELDS, AS IT HAD BECOME THE TIME FOR PLANTING. WITH BAG AND SEED, HE WALKED ALONG HIS FIELD SCATTERING THE SEED, AND SOME SEEDS FELL ALONG THE FOOTPATH.

THESE SEEDS COULD NOT FIND GOOD SOIL, SO THE BIRDS CAME AND ATE THEM UP.

SOME OF THE SEEDS FELL ON ROCKY GROUND, WHERE THERE WAS LITTLE SOIL.

118

THE SEEDS SPROUTED QUICKLY, BUT WHEN THE SUN CAME, THE WHEAT WAS SCORCHED AND DIED. OTHER SEEDS FELL AMONG THISTLES AND THE WEEDS CHOKED THE WHEAT.

FINALLY, SOME SEEDS FELL ON GOOD SOIL. FROM THERE, THEY TOOK ROOT AND BEGAN TO GROW. SOON THEY GREW STRONG AND TALL, AND THE SEEDS BORE FRUIT, YIELDING A HUNDRED-FOLD.

JESUS KNEW THAT PARABLES COULD BE DIFFICULT TO UNDERSTAND, SO WHEN THE DISCIPLES DID NOT KNOW WHAT THE STORY MEANT, JESUS EXPLAINED IT TO THEM.

The seed on the rock is like a man who, on hearing the Word, accepts it at once with joy, but as it strikes no root in him, he has no staying power, and when trouble comes, he falls away.

The seed sown among this-
tles represents the man who
hears the Word, but worldly
cares and the false glamour of
wealth choke it, and his faith
proves barren.

But the seed that comes upon
good soil is the man who hears
the Word and understands it. He
works at his faith and it grows.
His faith bears fruit.

HEAVEN IS LIKE A MUSTARD SEED, WHICH A MAN TOOK AND PUT INTO THE GROUND. AS A SEED, THE MUSTARD IS THE SMALLEST.

WHEN IT HAS GROWN, IT IS BIGGER THAN ANY PLANT—IT BECOMES A TREE, BIG ENOUGH FOR THE BIRDS TO SIT IN. WHAT LITTLE YOU DO ON EARTH FOR THE KINGDOM IS REWARDED BEYOND YOUR WILDEST DREAMS IN HEAVEN.

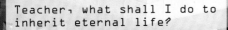

Teacher, what shall I do to inherit eternal life?

What is written in the law?

JESUS JOURNEYED ON TO THE NEXT TOWN. THERE, HE WENT INTO THE SYNAGOGUE. THERE WAS A LAWYER WHO STOOD UP TO PUT JESUS TO THE TEST.

Love the Lord and love your neighbor.

Correct.

But who is my neighbor?

116

A MAN WAS GOING DOWN FROM JERUSALEM TO JERICHO, AND HE FELL AMONG ROBBERS, WHO STRIPPED AND BEAT HIM, THEN DEPARTED, LEAVING HIM HALF DEAD ON THE SIDE OF THE ROAD.

NOW BY CHANCE, A PRIEST WAS GOING DOWN THAT ROAD, AND WHEN HE SAW THE INJURED MAN, HE THOUGHT TO HIMSELF, *THERE MUST BE DANGER NEARBY. I BETTER BE ON MY WAY.* SO HE PASSED BY ON THE OTHER SIDE, LEAVING THE INJURED MAN.

A LEVITE WALKED THE SAME PATH, AND WHEN HE CAME TO THE PLACE AND SAW THE INJURED MAN, HE PASSED BY ON THE OTHER SIDE.

THE NEXT MORNING, THE SAMARITAN TOOK OUT TWO DENARII AND GAVE THEM TO THE INNKEEPER, SAYING, "TAKE CARE OF HIM, AND WHATEVER MORE YOU SPEND, I WILL REPAY YOU WHEN I COME BACK."

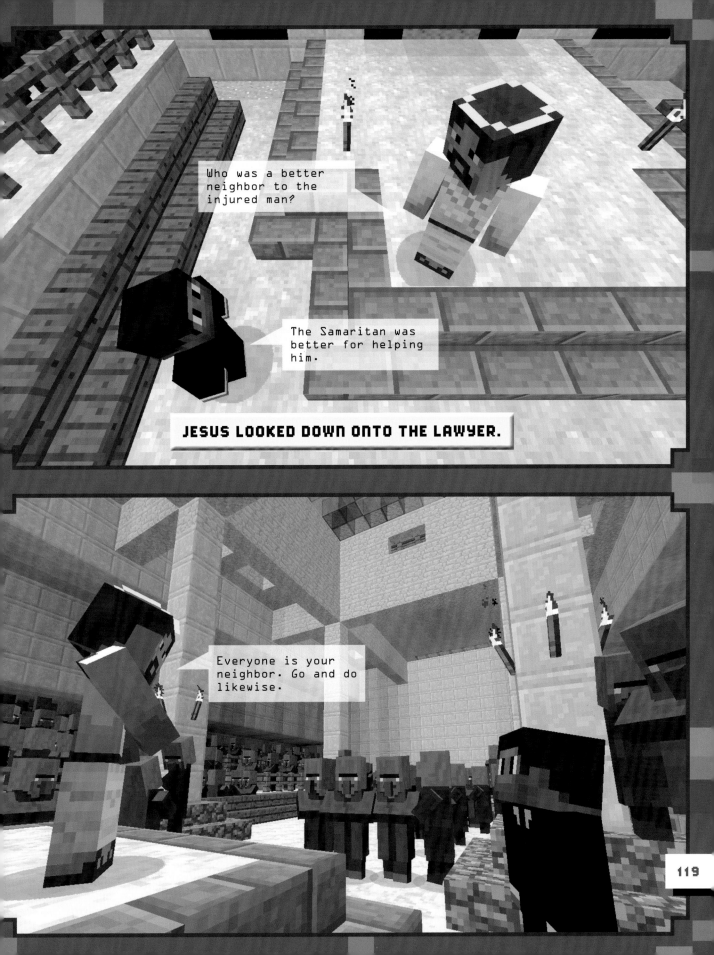

Who was a better
neighbor to the
injured man?

The Samaritan was
better for helping
him.

JESUS LOOKED DOWN ONTO THE LAWYER.

Everyone is your
neighbor. Go and do
likewise.

119

IF A MAN HAVING A HUNDRED SHEEP HAS LOST ONE OF THEM, DOES HE NOT LEAVE THE NINETY-NINE IN THE WILDERNESS, AND GO AFTER THE ONE WHICH IS LOST, UNTIL IT IS FOUND?

Rejoice with me, for I have found my sheep which was lost.

WHEN HE HAS FOUND IT, HE LAYS IT ON HIS SHOULDERS, REJOICING. AND WHEN HE COMES HOME, HE CALLS TOGETHER HIS FRIENDS AND HIS NEIGHBORS ASKING THEM TO SHARE IN HIS JOY. JUST SO, THERE WILL BE MORE JOY IN HEAVEN OVER ONE SINNER WHO REPENTS THAN OVER NINETY-NINE RIGHTEOUS PERSONS WHO NEED NO REPENTANCE.

JESUS FEEDS 5,000 PEOPLE

I think I'm beginning to understand how these parables work.

Master, the people must be hungry. We should let them go away to the nearest towns and find food.

IT WAS SUPPERTIME, AND THE DISCIPLES WANTED TO EXCUSE THEMSELVES TO GO EAT.

There is no need for them to go; give them what we have.

All we have here is five loaves and two fish.

JESUS KNEW HOW MUCH FOOD THEY HAD. HE WANTED TO SHOW THE DISCIPLES THAT IF THEY WERE CHARITABLE, GOD WOULD REWARD THEM WITH PLENTY.

JESUS GAVE THE LOAVES AND FISH TO THE DISCIPLES TO PASS OUT TO THE PEOPLE.

It is a miracle.

AS THE DISCIPLES PASSED OUT THE BREAD, THE BASKET DID NOT EMPTY. WHEN ONE PIECE WAS TAKEN, ANOTHER APPEARED.

ALL THE PEOPLE ATE TO THEIR HEARTS' CONTENT, AND THE SCRAPS LEFT OVER WERE ENOUGH TO FILL TWELVE GREAT BASKETS.

JESUS WALKS ON WATER

Is there no end to the amazing acts of Jesus? He's got quite an array of talents.

THE SUN WAS SETTING, AND JESUS TOLD THE DISCIPLES TO GO ON AHEAD OF HIM BY BOAT. JESUS THEN WENT UP THE HILLSIDE TO PRAY ALONE.

IT WAS GROWING LATE WHEN THE DISCIPLES SAW SOMETHING IN THE DISTANCE.

THE SUN WAS JUST RISING WHEN JESUS CAME TO THEM. HE WAS WALKING ON THE WATER!

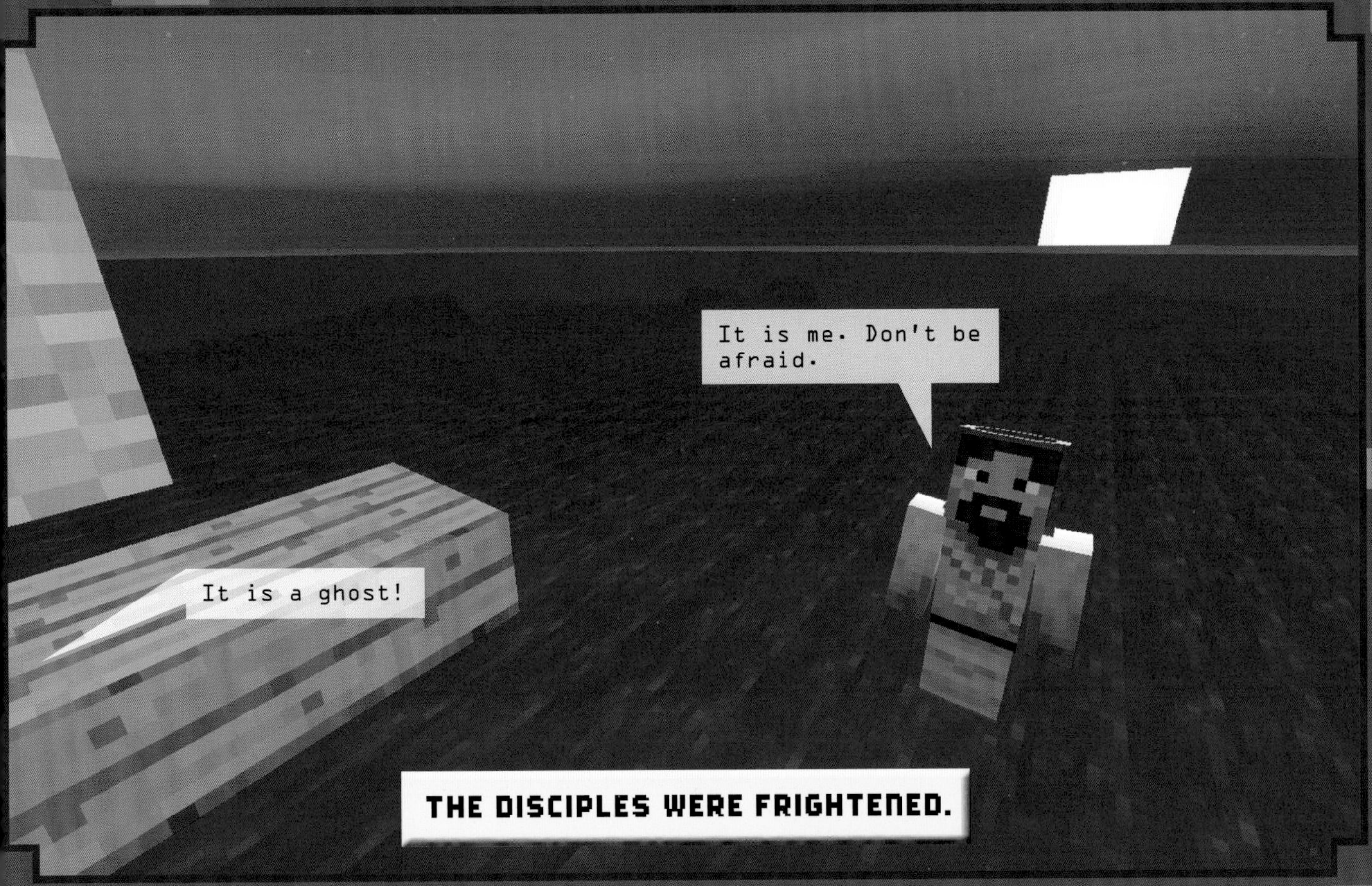
It is me. Don't be afraid.
It is a ghost!
THE DISCIPLES WERE FRIGHTENED.

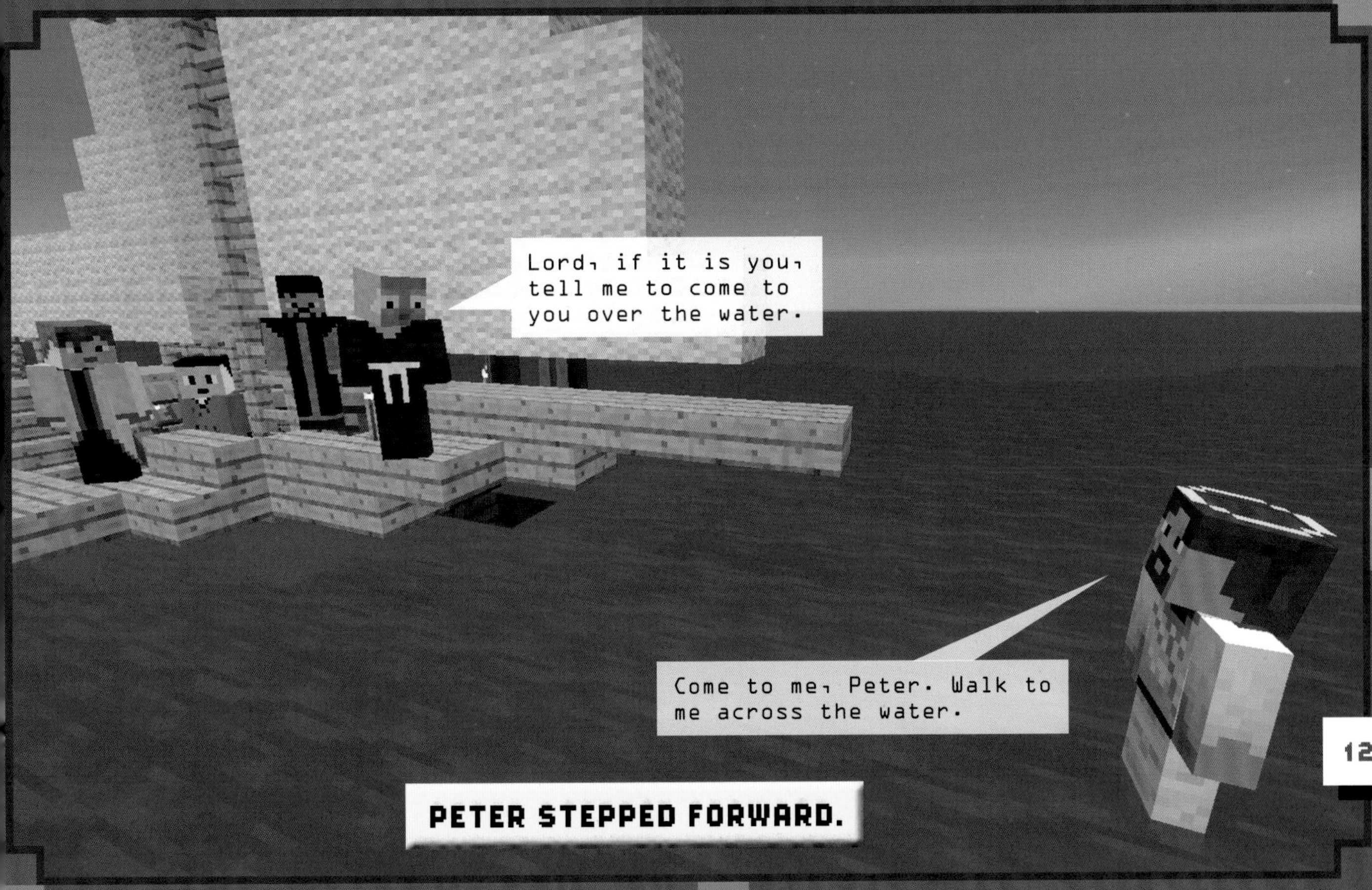
Lord, if it is you, tell me to come to you over the water.
Come to me, Peter. Walk to me across the water.
PETER STEPPED FORWARD.

Save me, Lord!

PETER STEPPED DOWN FROM THE BOAT, AND WALKED ON THE WATER TOWARD JESUS. WHEN PETER REALIZED WHAT HE WAS DOING, HE WAS STRUCK WITH FEAR AND BEGAN SINKING. HE CRIED OUT. JESUS TOOK HIS HAND AND HELD HIM UP.

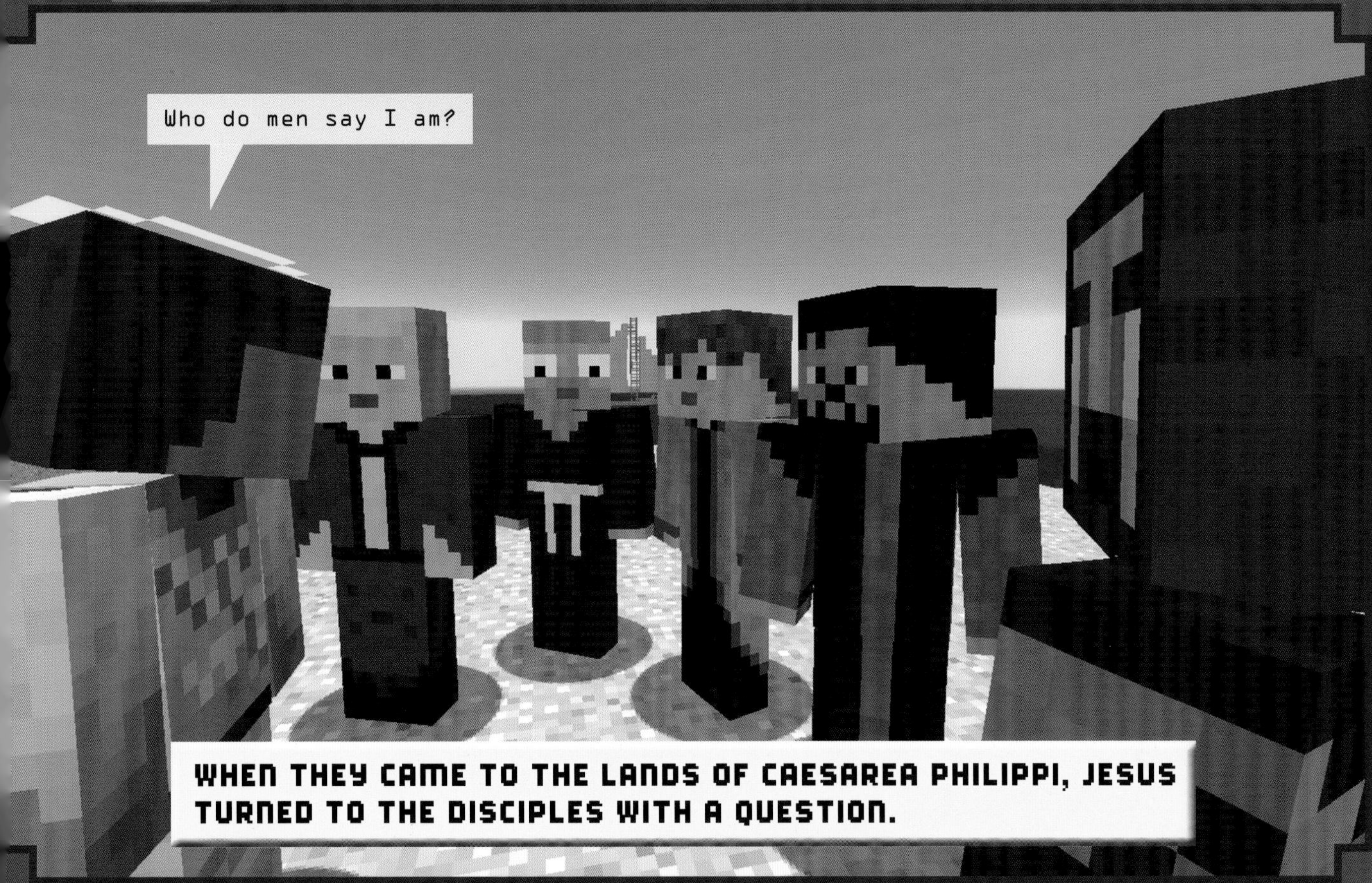
Who do men say I am?
WHEN THEY CAME TO THE LANDS OF CAESAREA PHILIPPI, JESUS TURNED TO THE DISCIPLES WITH A QUESTION.

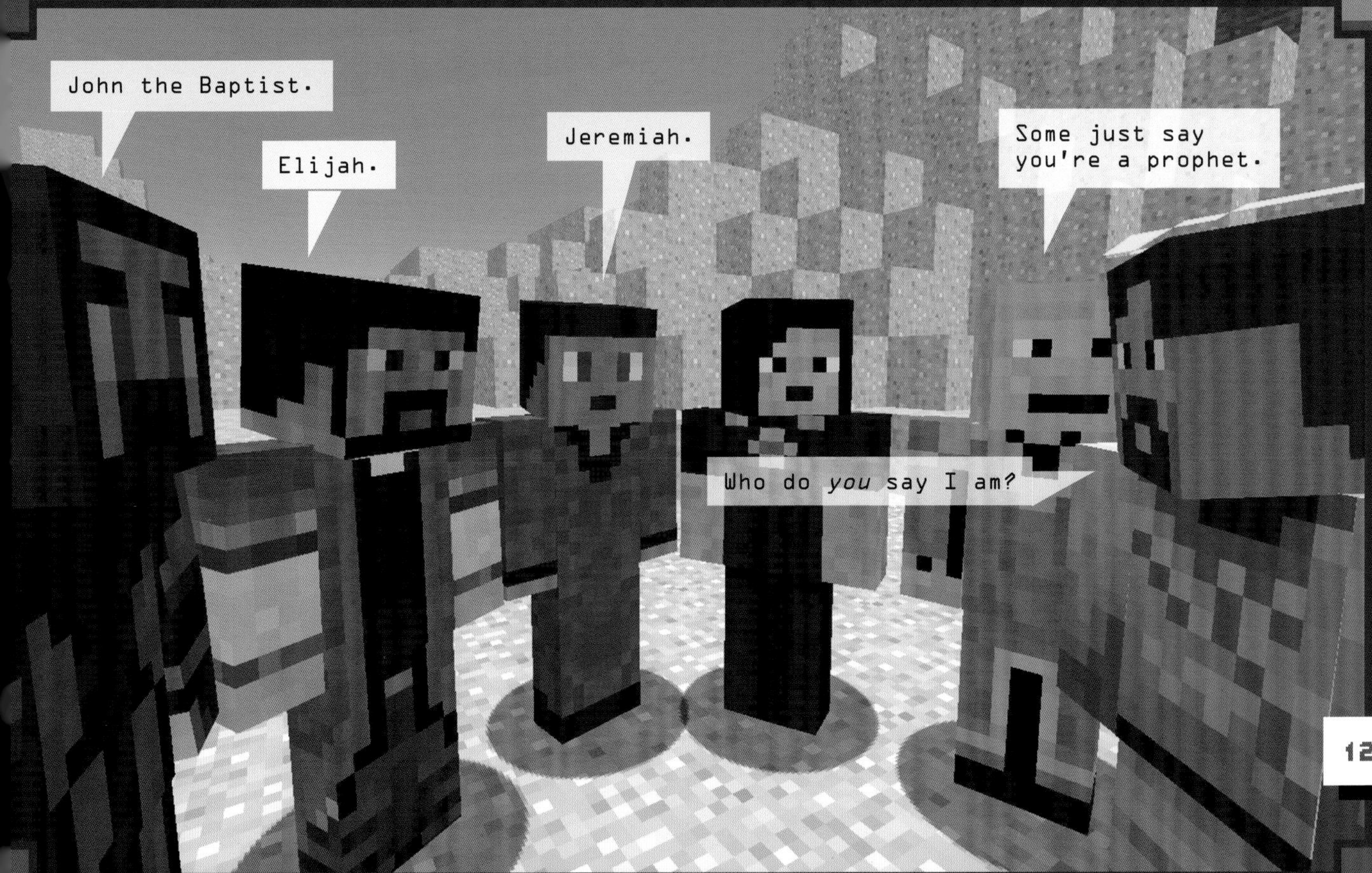
John the Baptist.
Elijah.
Jeremiah.
Some just say you're a prophet.
Who do *you* say I am?

You are the Messiah, the Son of the living God.

Peter, Son of Jonah, you are favored indeed! You did not learn that from mortal man; it was revealed to you by my Heavenly Father. And I say this to you: You are Peter, the Rock; and on this rock I will build my church.

THE DISCIPLES ALL HESITATED EXCEPT PETER. JESUS EXPLAINED THAT HE HAD TO GO TO JERUSALEM, AND THERE HE WOULD BE BEATEN AND PUT TO DEATH, BUT THEY SHOULD NOT FEAR; HE WOULD RISE AGAIN ON THE THIRD DAY.

JESUS RAISES LAZARUS

Wow! He's like that one kind of lizard . . .

The Jesus Lizard is named after him.

131

Thomas, please take a message to our Lord and ask him to come here.

A MAN NAMED LAZARUS WAS SICK. HE LIVED IN THE SAME TOWN AS MARY AND HER SISTER MARTHA.

IT WAS THE SAME MARY WHO ANOINTED THE LORD WITH PERFUME AND WIPED HIS FEET WITH HER HAIR. SHE WAS THE SISTER OF LAZARUS. MARY KNEW JESUS COULD HELP.

JESUS CHOSE NOT TO RUN IMMEDIATELY TO THEIR SIDE. HE STAYED TWO MORE DAYS IN THE PLACE WHERE HE WAS. HE WANTED TO SHOW THEM THE POWER OF THE LORD.

No, lately the Jews wish to stone you for what you teach.

Let us go to Judea again and to our friend Lazarus.

AFTER HE HAD WAITED THE TWO DAYS, JESUS INSTRUCTED HIS DISCIPLES.

Are there not twelve hours in the day? If anyone walks in the day, he does not stumble, because he sees the light of this world. But if one walks in the night, he stumbles, because the light is not in him.

JESUS SPOKE OF LAZARUS' DEATH.

Lazarus is dead. Nevertheless, let us go to him.

JESUS UNDERSTOOD THEIR CONFUSION. HE HAD NOT REVEALED HIS PLAN TO THEM.

Lord, if you had been here, my brother would not have died. But even now I know that whatever you ask of God, God will give you.

LAZARUS HAD ALREADY BEEN IN THE TOMB FOUR DAYS. MARTHA WENT AND MET HIM, BUT MARY STAYED IN THE HOUSE.

He who believes in me, though he may die, he shall live. And whoever lives and believes in me shall never die. Do you believe this?

Yes, Lord.

Whoever shall believe in me will not perish, but instead will have ever-lasting life.

Lord, if you had been here, my brother would not have died.

WHEN MARY FINALLY SAW JESUS, SHE ONCE AGAIN DROPPED TO HIS FEET AND BEGAN TO SOB. HE BROUGHT HER UP OFF THE GROUND AND DRIED HER TEARS WITH HIS SLEEVE.

Take away the stone. Now on this day you will see that the Son of God has power over death.

JESUS THEN WALKED OVER TO THE TOMB OF LAZARUS, AND IN A COMMANDING VOICE HE SPOKE.

Lazarus! Lazarus! Come rejoin
those who love you.

LAZARUS' TOMB WAS A SHALLOW CAVE, AND A LARGE STONE LAY AGAINST THE OPENING. THE MEN PUSHED AND PULLED ON THE STONE, AND SLOWLY IT MOVED TO THE SIDE.

137

LAZARUS STEPPED OUT OF THE TOMB, AND EVERYONE REJOICED!

JESUS' ENTRY INTO JERUSALEM

On to Jerusalem!

You got it! Enough groundwork has been laid. Jesus is ready to begin the end.

The end?

Go into the village that is just ahead of you,
and you will find a donkey tied to a post. Un-
tie it, and bring the donkey to me.

THE TIME CAME FOR JESUS TO COMPLETE HIS WORK, AND FOR THAT,
HE TURNED TOWARD JERUSALEM. HE SENT TWO DISCIPLES TO THE
NEAREST VILLAGE.

THIS WAS FORETOLD THROUGH THE PROPHET, SAYING, "TELL
THE DAUGHTER OF ZION, BEHOLD, YOUR KING IS COMING TO
YOU, MEEK, AND RIDING UPON A DONKEY."

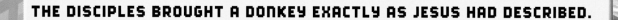

THE DISCIPLES BROUGHT A DONKEY EXACTLY AS JESUS HAD DESCRIBED.

THEY PUT THEIR GARMENTS OVER ITS BACK. THEN JESUS SAT UPON IT.

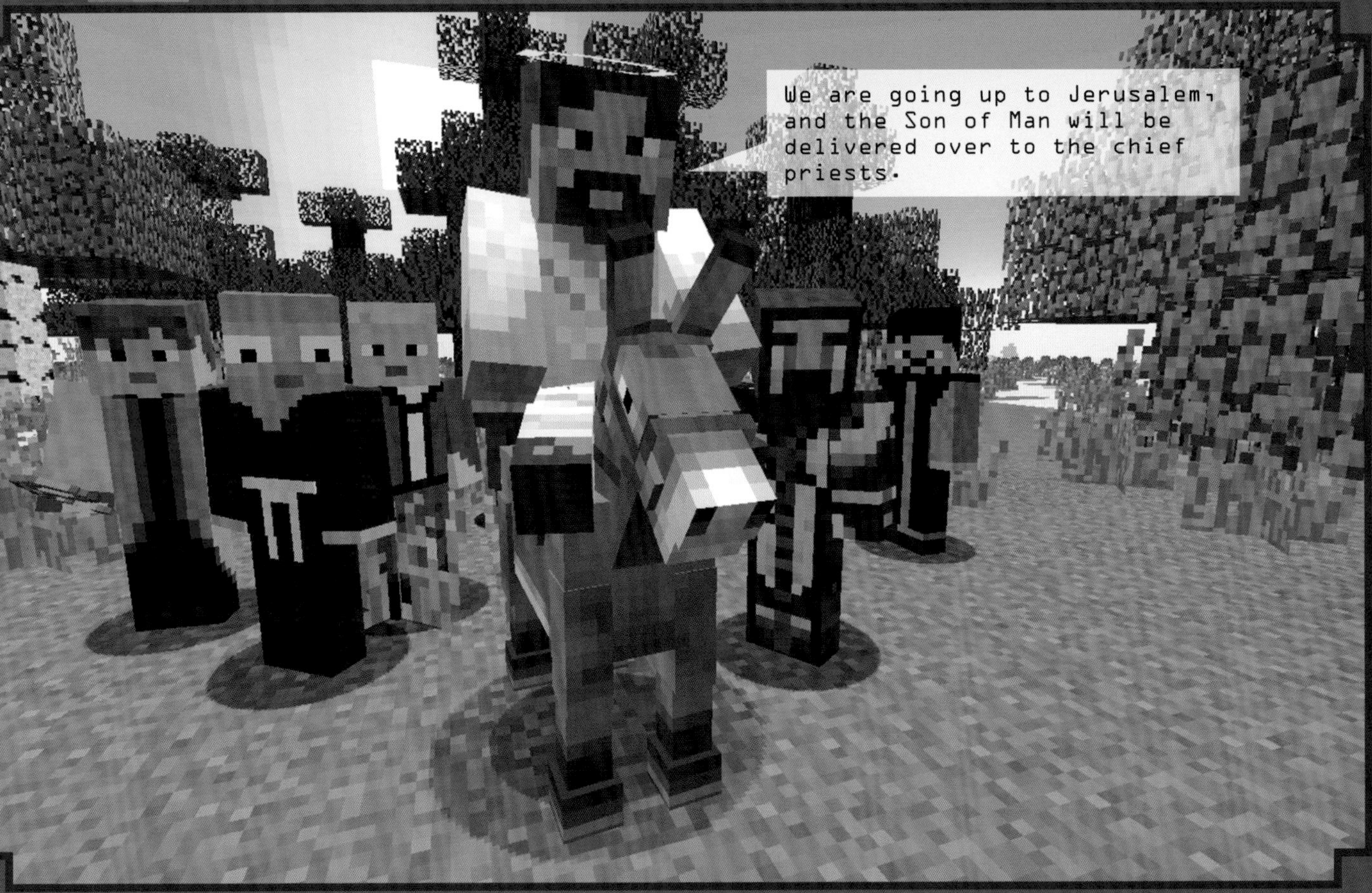
We are going up to Jerusalem, and the Son of Man will be delivered over to the chief priests.

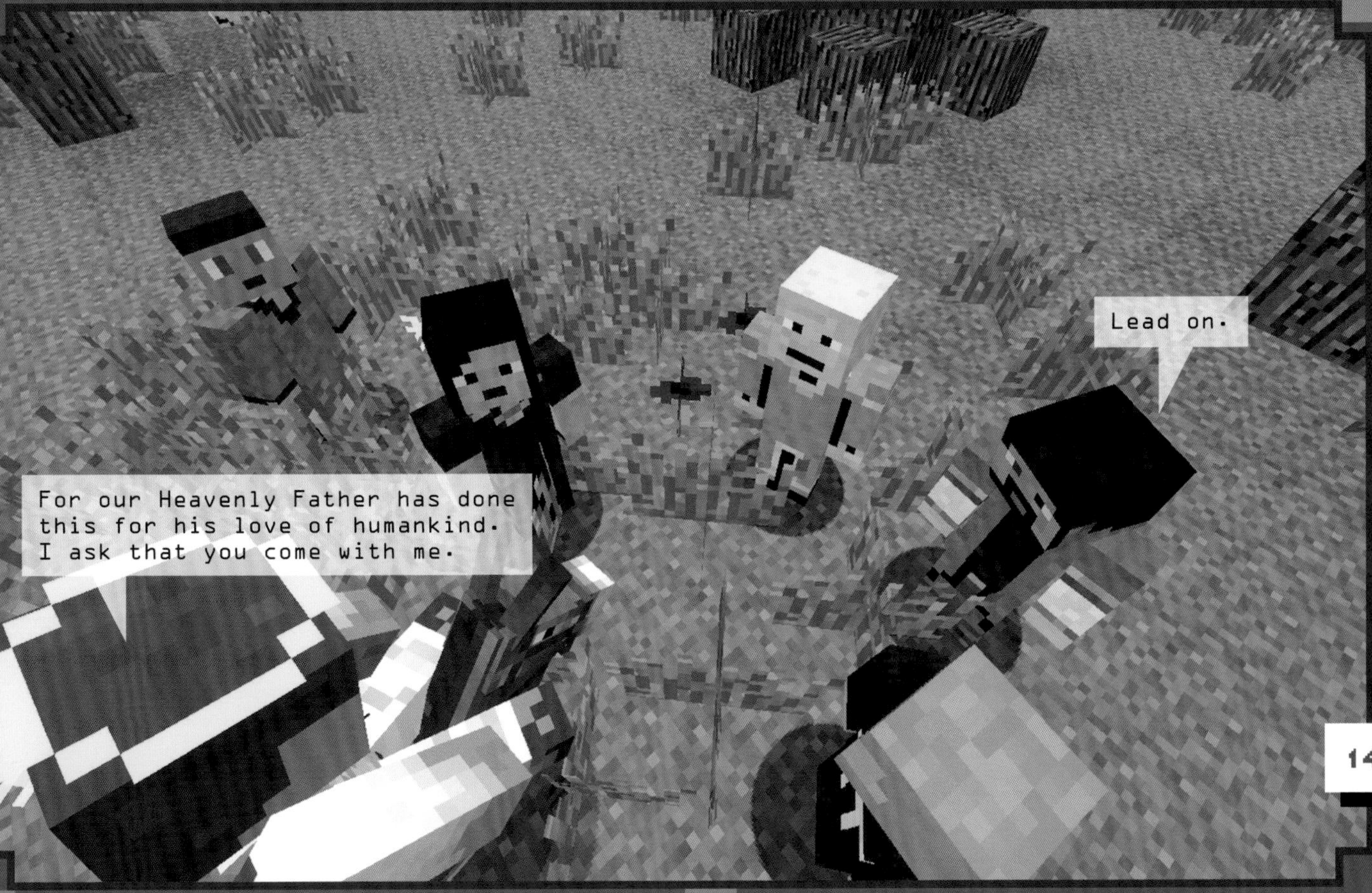
Lead on.
For our Heavenly Father has done this for his love of humankind. I ask that you come with me.

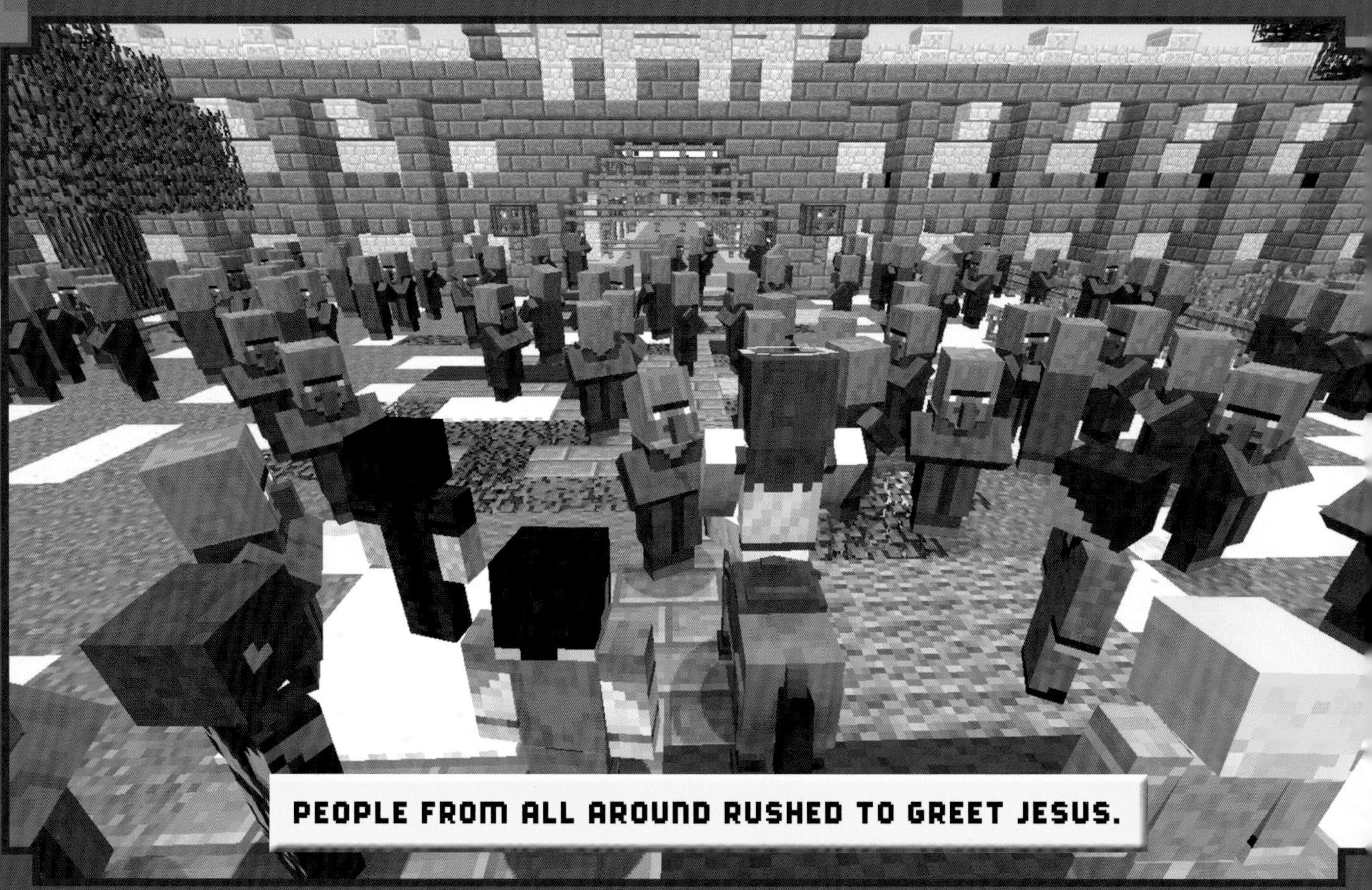
PEOPLE FROM ALL AROUND RUSHED TO GREET JESUS.

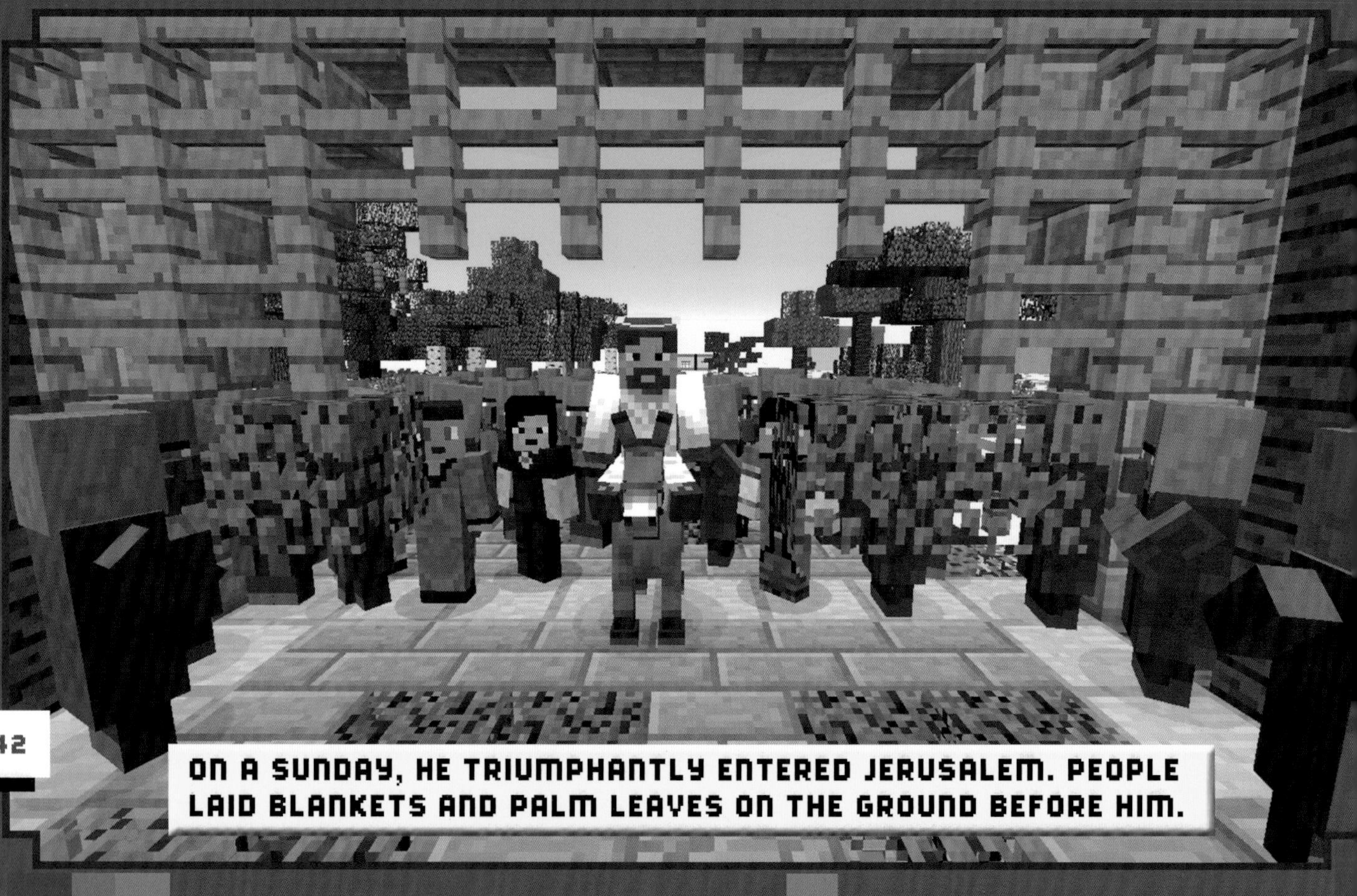
ON A SUNDAY, HE TRIUMPHANTLY ENTERED JERUSALEM. PEOPLE LAID BLANKETS AND PALM LEAVES ON THE GROUND BEFORE HIM.

THE CROWD WONDERED IF HE WAS REALLY JESUS FROM NAZARETH.

JESUS CHALLENGES THE AUTHORITIES

Now my Son will challenge the authorities that have corrupted my house and my kingdom.

ONCE JESUS ENTERED THE CITY, HE MADE HIS WAY TO THE GREAT TEMPLE. HE WAS STRUCK WITH OUTRAGE AT WHAT HE SAW. MEN OF ALL SORTS WERE TAKING MONEY FROM THE PEOPLE, SELLING WARES, AND USING THEM TO MAKE MONEY IN GOD'S HOLY TEMPLE. JESUS GRABBED A THICK ROPE AND APPROACHED THE MONEY CHANGERS.

Get out of my Father's house!

HE DROVE OUT ALL WHO WERE BUYING AND SELLING THERE.

Do you hear what these children are saying?

LATER, THE BLIND AND THE LAME CAME TO JESUS AT THE TEMPLE, AND HE HEALED THEM. THE PHARISEES BECAME INDIGNANT.

What do you think about the Messiah? Whose son is he?

The son of David.

THE PHARISEES LAID PLANS TO TRAP JESUS.

So the Messiah is not both man and God.

How is it then that David, speaking by the Spirit, calls the Messiah Lord? For he says, "The Lord said to my Lord: Sit at my right hand until I put your enemies under your feet." If then David calls him "Lord," how can he be his son?

Which is the greatest commandment?

He was man and God combined.

Love the Lord your God with all your heart and with all your soul and with all your mind.

You now understand.

THE PHARISEES TRIED AGAIN.

Teacher, we know that you are a man of integrity and that you teach the way of God. Tell us, is it right to pay the imperial tax to Caesar or not?

You hypocrites, show me the coin used for paying the tax.

THE PHARISEES FAILED TO TRAP JESUS BY JEWISH LAW, SO THEY SENT THEIR DISCIPLES TO TRY AND TRAP HIM ONCE MORE UNDER ROMAN LAW.

Whose image is this? And whose inscription?

Caesar's.

Then render unto Caesar what is Caesar's and to God what is God's.

THEY BROUGHT HIM A DENARIUS AND HE ASKED THEM A QUESTION.

You must be careful to do everything they tell you. But do not do what they do, for they do not practice what they preach.

JESUS GAVE THE CROWD AND HIS DISCIPLES A WARNING ABOUT THE PHARISEES.

Everything they do is done for people to see: they love the place of honor at banquets and the most important seats in the synagogues; they love to be called Rabbi by others.

You are not to be called Rabbi, for you have one Teacher. And do not call anyone on Earth father, for you have one Father, and he is in heaven. For those who exalt themselves will be humbled, and those who humble themselves will be exalted.

JESUS' FINAL DAYS

The final moment has arrived. Salvation has come and my plan will be fulfilled.

It's not going to be easy, is it?

Yes, his greatest challenges are ahead of him, and his divine strength will be needed.

Where do you want us to make preparations for the Passover supper?

I am going to celebrate the Passover with my disciples.

ON THE FIRST DAY OF THE FESTIVAL OF UNLEAVENED BREAD, THE DISCIPLES CAME TO JESUS AND ASKED ABOUT THE PASSOVER MEAL.

One of you will betray me.

Surely you don't mean me, Rabbi?

The one who has dipped his hand into the bowl with me will betray me. Woe to that man who betrays the Son of Man! It would be better for him if he had not been born.

151

WHEN EVENING CAME, WHILE THEY WERE EATING, JESUS SPOKE OF AN ATROCITY. THEN JUDAS, KNOWING HE WAS THE GUILTY ONE, TRIED TO ACCUSE THE OTHERS.

Take this bread and eat it; this is my body. Take this cup and drink from it, all of you. This is my blood of the covenant, which is poured out for many, for the forgiveness of sins.

JESUS TOOK BREAD AND DIVIDED IT AMONGST THE DISCIPLES. THEN HE TOOK A CUP.

Who is it you want?

Jesus of Nazareth.

WHEN HE FINISHED PRAYING, JESUS LEFT WITH HIS DISCIPLES AND CROSSED THE KIDRON VALLEY. THERE WAS A GARDEN, AND HE AND SOME OF THE DISCIPLES WENT TO IT TO PRAY AND REFLECT. JUDAS, WHO BETRAYED HIM, SOON CAME TO THE GARDEN, GUIDING SOLDIERS FROM THE CHIEF PRIESTS AND THE PHARISEES. THEY CARRIED TORCHES, LANTERNS, AND WEAPONS.

JUDAS THEN CAME UP TO JESUS AND KISSED HIM ON THE CHEEK. THIS SIGNALED TO THE GUARDS WHICH ONE WAS JESUS.

If you are looking for me, then let these men go.

THE GUARDS STEPPED FORWARD.

Put your sword away! Peter, know that those who live by the sword, die by the sword.

154

THEN PETER, WHO HAD A SWORD, DREW IT AND STRUCK THE HIGH PRIEST'S SERVANT, CUTTING OFF HIS RIGHT EAR. JESUS IMMEDIATELY TOLD HIS MEN TO STAND THEIR GROUND.

THEN JESUS WAS ARRESTED.

Is it true, you and your disciples speak falsely?

I have spoken openly to the world.

PETER FOLLOWED JESUS AND THE OFFICIALS TO THE HIGH PRIEST, BUT HAD TO WAIT OUTSIDE.

155

Is this the way you answer the high priest?

ONE OF THE OFFICIALS SLAPPED JESUS IN THE FACE. HE WOULD BE TAKEN BEFORE THE ROMAN GOVERNOR.

This man has been leading our people astray by telling them not to pay their taxes to the Roman government and by claiming he is the Messiah.

THE HIGH PRIEST BROUGHT HIM BEFORE PONTIUS PILATE, THE ROMAN GOVERNOR. THE PHARISEES BEGAN TO STATE THEIR CASE AGAINST JESUS TO THE GOVERNOR.

My kingdom is not of this world. If it was, do you think my followers would have let the Pharisees hand me over? I come willingly.

They want me to have you killed. Why?

PILATE TOOK JESUS TO HIS OFFICE TO QUESTION HIM.

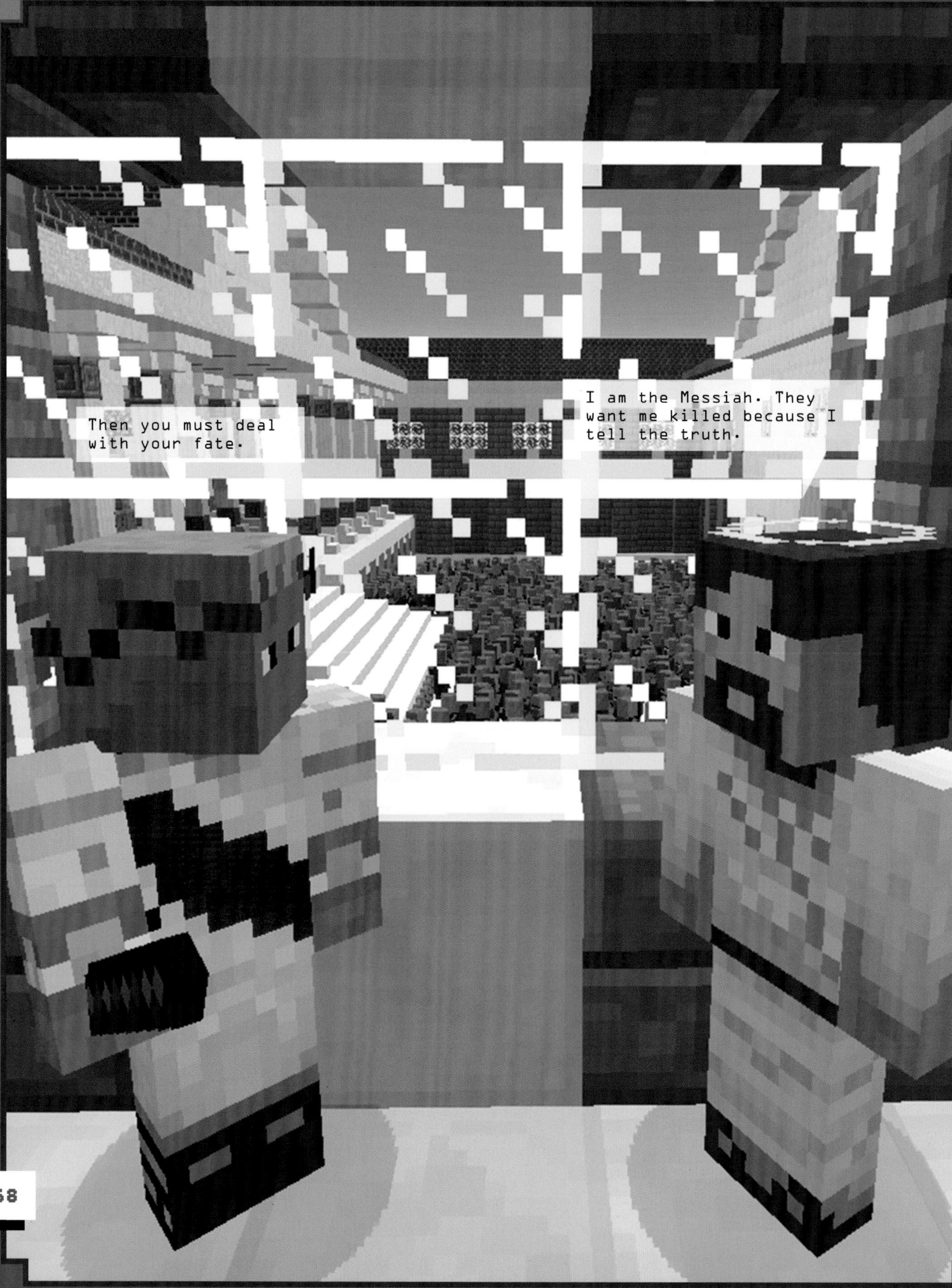
Then you must deal with your fate.
I am the Messiah. They want me killed because I tell the truth.

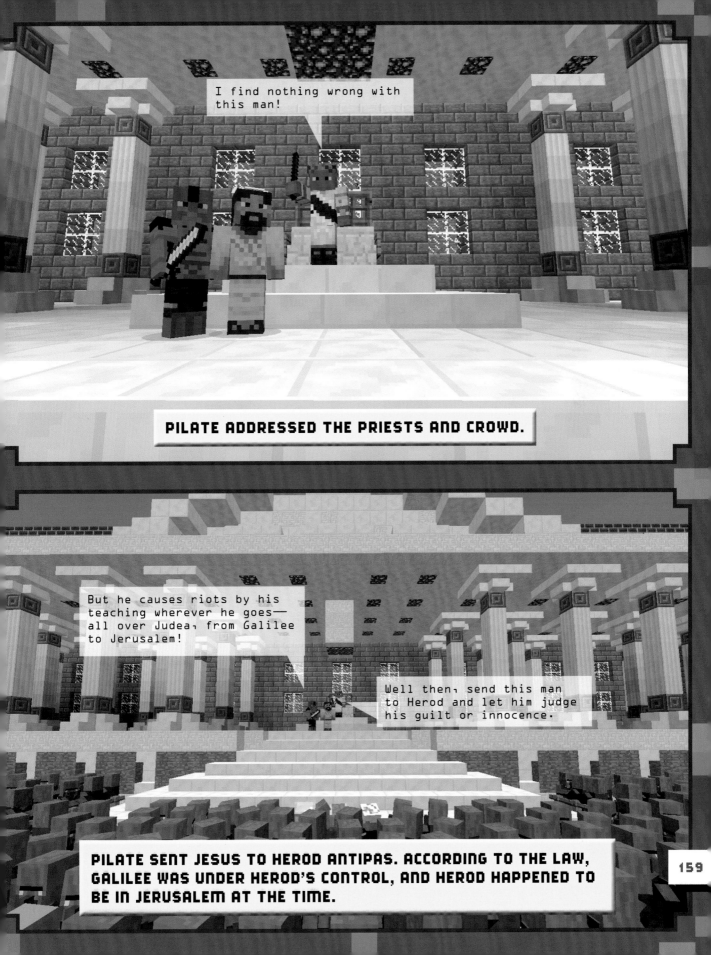

I find nothing wrong with this man!

PILATE ADDRESSED THE PRIESTS AND CROWD.

But he causes riots by his teaching wherever he goes—all over Judea, from Galilee to Jerusalem!

Well then, send this man to Herod and let him judge his guilt or innocence.

PILATE SENT JESUS TO HEROD ANTIPAS. ACCORDING TO THE LAW, GALILEE WAS UNDER HEROD'S CONTROL, AND HEROD HAPPENED TO BE IN JERUSALEM AT THE TIME.

Are you the one that can perform miracles? If you are, then do one for me. Prove to me that you're no fool— walk across my swimming pool.

What's wrong with him? He should speak.

HEROD II WAS DELIGHTED TO MEET JESUS, BECAUSE HE HAD HEARD MUCH ABOUT HIM. HE ASKED JESUS QUESTION AFTER QUESTION, BUT JESUS REFUSED TO ANSWER. HE WAS FINALLY SENT BACK TO PILATE.

Nothing this man has done calls for the death penalty. So I will have him flogged, and then I will release him. I offer you instead this criminal Barabbas. Will you take Barabbas the turncoat and murderer, or Jesus?

PILATE CALLED EVERYONE TOGETHER AND ANNOUNCED HIS VERDICT.

Kill him!

A MIGHTY ROAR ROSE FROM THE CROWD, AND WITH ONE VOICE THEY SHOUTED, "KILL HIM, AND RELEASE BARABBAS TO US!"

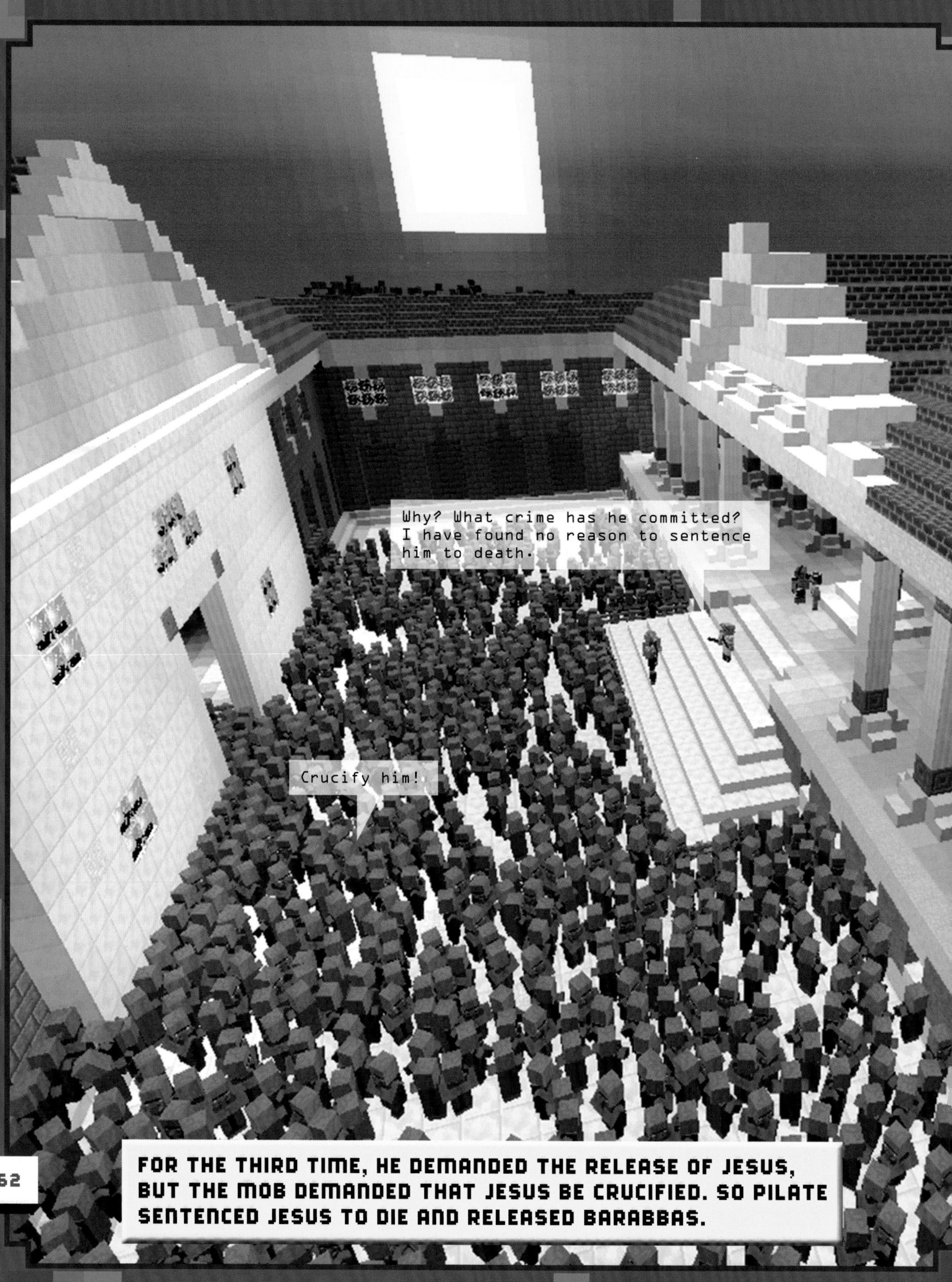
Why? What crime has he committed? I have found no reason to sentence him to death.
Crucify him!
FOR THE THIRD TIME, HE DEMANDED THE RELEASE OF JESUS, BUT THE MOB DEMANDED THAT JESUS BE CRUCIFIED. SO PILATE SENTENCED JESUS TO DIE AND RELEASED BARABBAS.

JESUS WAS HANDED OVER TO THE ROMAN SOLDIERS. HE WAS THEN STRIPPED AND BEATEN WITH THIRTY-NINE LASHINGS, AND A CROWN OF THORNS WAS PLACED ON HIS HEAD.

NEXT, JESUS CARRIED HIS CROSS THROUGH TOWN, HEADING OUT TO A MOUNT CALLED THE SKULL.

AT THE EDGE OF THE CITY, JESUS COULD NO LONGER BEAR THE WEIGHT OF THE CROSS AND COLLAPSED. A MAN NAMED PETER, WHO WAS FROM CYRENE, HAPPENED TO BE COMING IN FROM THE COUNTRYSIDE. THE SOLDIERS SEIZED HIM AND PUT THE CROSS ON HIM, MAKING HIM CARRY IT BEHIND JESUS.

OTHER CRIMINALS WERE LED OUT TO BE EXECUTED ALONG WITH JESUS. WHEN THEY CAME TO THE SKULL, THE ROMANS NAILED JESUS TO THE CROSS, AND SET IT UPRIGHT. THE CRIMINALS WERE ALSO HUNG ON CROSSES—ONE TO THE RIGHT OF JESUS, AND ONE TO THE LEFT.

So you're the Messiah, are you? Prove it by saving yourself—and us, too, while you're at it!

We deserve to die for our crimes, but this man hasn't done anything wrong. Jesus, remember me when you come into your Kingdom.

I assure you, today you will be with me in paradise.

ONE OF THE CRIMINALS HANGING BESIDE JESUS STARTED TO MOCK HIM AND SAY MEAN THINGS, BUT THE OTHER CRIMINAL PROTESTED.

THE DEATH AND RESURRECTION OF JESUS

I can't look. I have to turn away.

Don't worry. My Son's mission will be fulfilled.

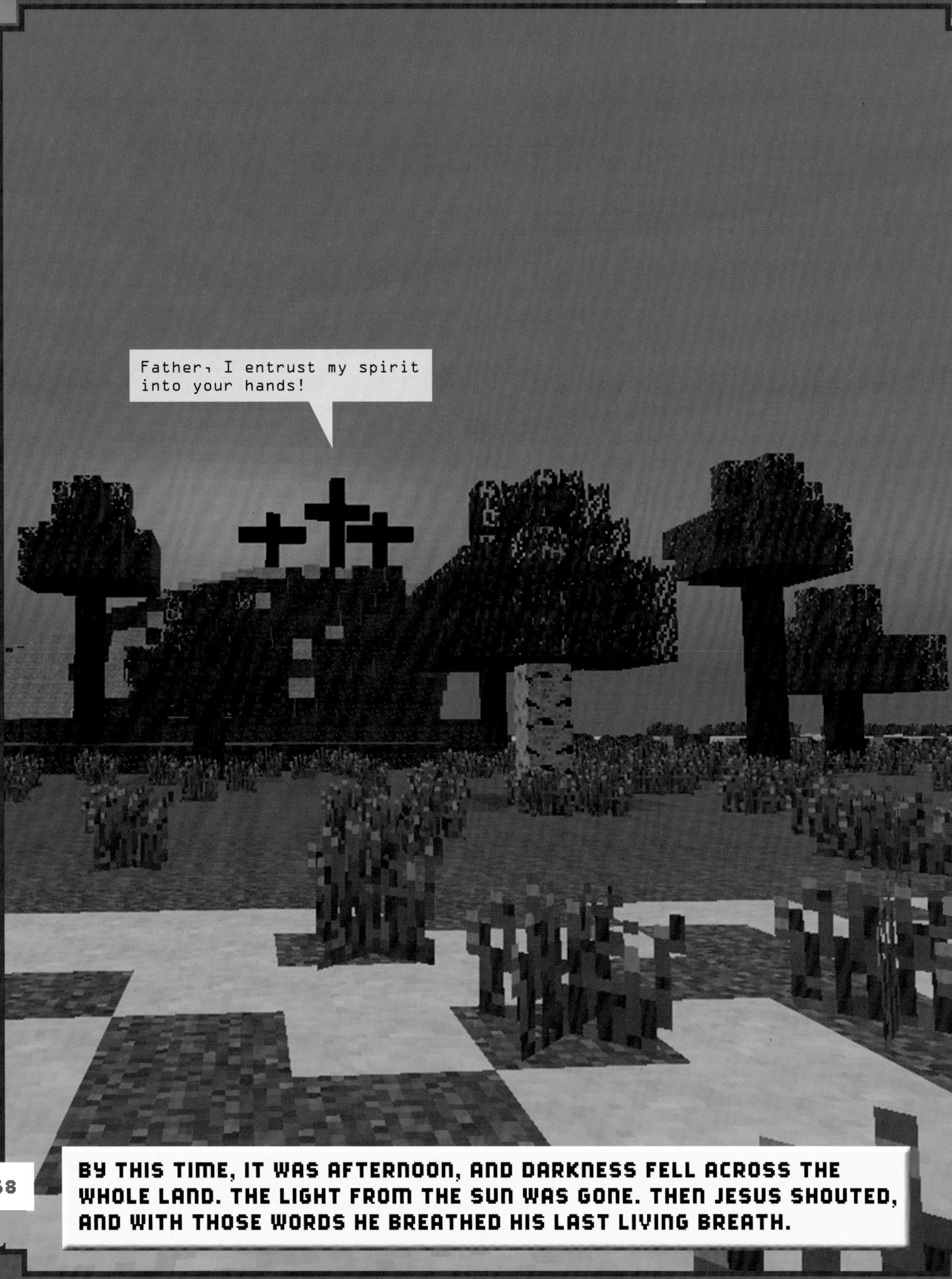
Father, I entrust my spirit into your hands!
BY THIS TIME, IT WAS AFTERNOON, AND DARKNESS FELL ACROSS THE WHOLE LAND. THE LIGHT FROM THE SUN WAS GONE. THEN JESUS SHOUTED, AND WITH THOSE WORDS HE BREATHED HIS LAST LIVING BREATH.

A RIGHTEOUS MAN NAMED JOSEPH WAS A MEMBER OF THE JEWISH HIGH COUNCIL, BUT HE HAD NOT AGREED WITH THE DECISION OF THE OTHER RELIGIOUS LEADERS. HE DID NOT WANT JESUS' BODY TO BE FURTHER DISGRACED, SO HE WENT TO PILATE AND ASKED FOR IT.

THEN, PETER WRAPPED THE BODY IN A LONG SHEET OF LINEN CLOTH AND LAID IT IN A NEW TOMB THAT HAD BEEN CARVED OUT OF ROCK. BY NIGHTFALL, JESUS' BODY HAD BEEN PLACED INSIDE AND THE TOMB HAD BEEN SEALED, WHILE SOLDIERS STOOD GUARD.

ON THE FIRST DAY OF THE WEEK, VERY EARLY IN THE MORNING,
MARY, JESUS'S MOTHER, AND MARY MAGDALENE TOOK THE
SPICES THEY HAD PREPARED AND WENT TO THE TOMB. ODDLY,
THEY FOUND THE STONE ROLLED AWAY FROM THE TOMB, AND
WHEN THEY ENTERED, THEY DID NOT FIND THE BODY OF THE
LORD JESUS.

SUDDENLY, TWO MEN IN CLOTHES THAT GLEAMED LIKE LIGHTNING STOOD IN FRONT OF THEM.

It's true, Jesus has risen!

Yeah right!

WHEN THEY REACHED THE VILLAGE, THE WOMEN TOLD ALL THAT THEY SAW.

PETER RAN TO THE TOMB. HE SAW THE STRIPS OF LINEN LYING BY THEMSELVES.

PETER, MOTHER MARY, AND MARY MAGDALENE RETURNED TO JERUSALEM TO BRING THE GOOD NEWS TO THE OTHER DISCIPLES.

JESUS ASCENDS TO HEAVEN

My Son is finally
coming home!

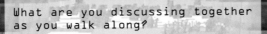

What are you discussing together
as you walk along?

THAT SAME DAY, TWO OF JESUS' FOLLOWERS WERE GOING TO A VILLAGE
CALLED EMMAUS, ABOUT SEVEN MILES FROM JERUSALEM. JESUS HIMSELF
CAME UP AND WALKED ALONG WITH THEM, BUT THEY WERE KEPT FROM
RECOGNIZING HIM.

ONE OF THEM, CLEOPAS, SPOKE TO JESUS WITHOUT KNOWING IT WAS HIM.

How foolish you are, and how slow to believe all that the prophets have spoken! Did not the Messiah have to suffer these things and then enter his glory?

Stay with us, for it is nearly evening— the day is almost over.

177

AS THEY APPROACHED THE HOUSE TO WHICH THEY WERE GOING, THEY URGED JESUS TO COME WITH THEM. HE AGREED TO HAVE SUPPER WITH THEM.

WHILE JESUS WAS AT THE TABLE WITH THEM, HE TOOK BREAD, GAVE THANKS, BROKE IT, AND BEGAN TO SHARE IT WITH THEM. THEN, THEIR EYES OPENED WIDE, AS THEY REALIZED THAT THEY RECOGNIZED JESUS, BUT HE QUICKLY DISAPPEARED FROM THEIR SIGHT.

THEY RETURNED, AT ONCE, TO JERUSALEM. THERE THEY FOUND THE ELEVEN APOSTLES AND TOLD THEM WHAT HAPPENED.

Peace be with you.

WHILE THEY WERE TALKING ABOUT THIS, JESUS HIMSELF APPEARED AMONG THEM.

Touch me and see—a ghost does not have flesh and bones, as you see I have.

THEY WERE STARTLED AND FRIGHTENED.

THOMAS WANTED PROOF THAT IT WAS TRULY JESUS. JESUS SHOWED THEM HIS HANDS AND FEET, ALTHOUGH THEY STILL DID NOT BELIEVE HIM.

I told you everything must be fulfilled that is written about me in the Law of Moses, the Prophets, and the Psalms. This is what is written: "The Messiah will suffer and rise from the dead on the third day, and repentance for the forgiveness of sins will be preached in his name to all nations, beginning at Jerusalem. You are witnesses of these things. I am going to send you out to preach the good news as my Father has promised."

JESUS OPENED THEIR MINDS SO THEY COULD UNDERSTAND THE SCRIPTURES.

It is time for me to leave you now. Go forth with my blessing.

AFTER HE LED THEM OUT TO THE VICINITY OF BETHANY, HE LIFTED UP HIS HANDS AND BLESSED THEM.

I must go join my Father, but you must carry on what I have begun here. I have taught you well, now carry on my message.

JESUS THEN LEFT AND ASCENDED INTO HEAVEN.

THE APOSTLES RETURNED TO JERUSALEM WITH GREAT JOY. THEY SAT AT THE TEMPLE FOR MANY DAYS PRAISING GOD.

Glory be to the Highest, peace on Earth and goodwill towards men.

THE APOSTLES CARRIED OUT HIS WISHES, AND LET ALL THE PEOPLE OF THE WORLD KNOW THE GOOD WORD. FOR GOD SO LOVED THE WORLD THAT HE GAVE HIS ONE AND ONLY SON, SO THAT WHOEVER BELIEVES IN HIM SHALL HAVE ETERNAL LIFE.

THE REPLACEMENT
FOR JUDAS

If they are to carry on the teachings of Jesus, they're going to need more apostles.

AFTER JESUS ASCENDED TO HEAVEN, THE APOSTLES RETURNED TO JERUSALEM.

WHEN THEY ARRIVED, THEY WENT UPSTAIRS TO THEIR APARTMENT.

PRESENT WERE: BARNABUS, PHILIP, SIMON A. THOMAS, ANDREW, JAMES, PETER, MATTHEW, BARTHOLOMEW, JOHN, AND SIMON Z.

Brothers and sisters, the scriptures had to be fulfilled.

IN THOSE DAYS, PETER STOOD UP AMONG THE BELIEVERS.

The Holy Spirit spoke long ago through David and said that Judas would betray Jesus.

It is written in the book of Psalms: Let there be another to take the place of leadership and restore the holy 12.

WE SHALL CHOOSE ONE WHO HAS BEEN WITH US FROM THE BEGINNING.

TWO MEN WERE NOMINATED: JOSEPH AND MATTHIAS.

THEN THEY PRAYED.

Lord, show us which of these two you have chosen.

188

MATTHIAS WAS CHOSEN.

THE HOLY SPIRIT COMES

So now the apostles will become even more spiritually enlightened?

WHEN THE DAY OF PENTECOST CAME, THE APOSTLES WERE ALL TOGETHER, PRAYING.

SUDDENLY, THEY SAW WHAT SEEMED TO BE TONGUES OF FIRE.

Lauda Deum.

Lob gott.

Hála Istennek!

THE FIRE CAME TO REST ON EACH OF THEM. THEY BECAME FILLED WITH THE HOLY SPIRIT, AND EACH BEGAN TO SPEAK IN FOREIGN LANGUAGES.

EXPANDING TRADE ROUTES ALLOWED PEOPLE OF MANY NATIONS TO TRAVEL TO GALILEE.

WHEN THE FOREIGNERS HEARD THE APOSTLES SPEAKING THE LANGUAGES OF THEIR HOMELANDS, THEY STOOD IN BEWILDERMENT.

UTTERLY AMAZED, THEY ASKED HOW.

Aren't all these men Galileans? How do they know so many languages?

THE PEOPLE WERE EXCITED BY THIS NEWS.

Jesus died for our sins. If you believe in him, you will have eternal life.

191

Repent and be baptized in the name of Jesus Christ for the forgiveness of your sins.

Brothers! What is it that we must do to be saved?

THEY ASKED WHAT TO DO.

THOSE WHO ACCEPTED THE MESSAGE WERE BAPTIZED. NEARLY 3,000 WERE SAVED THAT DAY.

My friends, listen to the truth. Jesus was a man accredited by God.

He performed miracles, wonders, and signs, which you yourselves know.

SEEING THE CROWD EAGER TO HEAR THE MESSAGE, PETER STOOD UP.

He was handed over to wicked men and nailed to the cross where he died.

But God raised him from the dead, because God has power over death. So shall you, if you believe.

THE NEW BELIEVERS FOLLOWED THE APOSTLES.

THEY SOLD POSSESSIONS AND GAVE TO THE NEEDY.

THEY MET EVERY DAY TO TALK.

THEY BROKE BREAD IN THEIR HOMES.

THEY PRAISED GOD IN SONG.

AND THEIR NUMBERS GREW DAILY.

THE CHURCH'S FIRST MARTYR

Those who believe are strong in the faith and have no fear proclaiming the word of God. Jesus, your name is exalted above all Angels and men. Praise be to you!

She needs her daily bread!

Have her bring her husband and we will give him the bread.

She has no husband.

IN THOSE EARLY DAYS OF THE CHURCH, THE HELLENISTIC FOLLOWERS OF CHRIST OFTEN COMPLAINED AGAINST THE HEBRAIC FOLLOWERS OF CHRIST. THIS TIME, THE HELLENISTIC FOLLOWERS ARGUED THAT THE HEBREWS IGNORED WIDOWS WHEN GIVING CHARITY.

We will choose seven to lead Jerusalem's Church.

THE COMPLAINTS WERE PASSED ON TO THE TWELVE DISCIPLES.

THE DISCIPLES DECIDED TO SELECT A LEADER TO HANDLE THE DAY-TO-DAY ISSUES.

THE BEST AMONG THE SEVEN MEN CHOSEN TO LEAD WAS A MAN BY THE NAME OF STEPHEN.

I will continue the work here. You and the other disciples can go into the world and spread the Word.

STEPHEN TOOK THE LEAD AND WENT OUT AMONG THE PEOPLE, PREACHING GOD'S MESSAGE.

MEMBERS OF THE SYNAGOGUE TRIED TO RATTLE STEPHEN, AS THE NEW CHURCH LEADER, AND BEGAN TO ARGUE WITH HIM.

THEY COULD NOT WIN AGAINST THE WISDOM OF STEPHEN, AND STORMED OFF IN A RAGE, KNOWING THEY WOULD HAVE TO RESORT TO OTHER TACTICS.

We want you to bear false witness. We will pay you.

MEMBERS OF THE SYNAGOGUE PERSUADED PEOPLE TO LIE AGAINST STEPHEN.

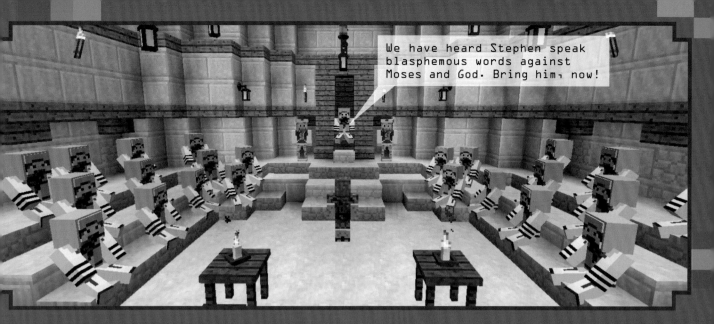

We have heard Stephen speak blasphemous words against Moses and God. Bring him, now!

SOLDIERS ARRESTED STEPHEN, AND DRAGGED HIM OFF.

HE STOOD BEFORE THE LAW.

> This fellow never stops speaking against the law.

PEOPLE PRODUCED FALSE CLAIMS AGAINST STEPHEN TO THE COURTS.

> We heard him say that Jesus will destroy the temple.

ALL THE SANHEDRIN LOOKED INTENSELY AT STEPHEN.

Are these charges true?

THE HIGH PRIEST ASKED STEPHEN TO ACCOUNT FOR THE ACCUSATIONS.

"The God of glory appeared to our father Abraham. . . ."

STEPHEN RETOLD THE OLD TESTAMENT EXACTLY AS IT WAS WRITTEN, SHOWING THAT HE WAS AN EXPERT IN THE LAW.

You stiff-necked people! Your hearts and ears are still closed. You are just like your ancestors—you always resist the Holy Spirit! Was there ever a prophet you did not persecute? You even killed those who predicted the coming of the Righteous One. Then you betrayed and murdered Him! This is what the Old Testament has predicted, and you still will not listen.

THE SANHEDRIN WERE FURIOUS AND GNASHED THEIR TEETH AT HIM.

Look, I see Heaven open.

BUT STEPHEN WAS FILLED WITH THE HOLY SPIRIT.

The Son of Man is there. He is sitting at the right hand of God.

AT THIS, THE PRIESTS COVERED THEIR EARS AND YELLED SO THEY DIDN'T HAVE TO LISTEN.

THE PRIESTS AND SADDUCEES COULD TAKE NO MORE OF STEPHEN'S TALK AND RUSHED AT HIM.

THEY STONED STEPHEN. A MAN NAMED SAUL LOOKED ON AT THE ATROCITY, BUT KNEW HE COULD NOT DO ANYTHING TO STOP IT.

Lord, do not hold this sin against them!

PETER BEGINS
THE GREAT WORKS

Jesus' right-hand man
is stepping up.

ONE DAY, PETER AND JOHN WERE GOING UP TO THE TEMPLE.

WHEN THE MAN SAW PETER, HE CALLED OUT.

Do you have any money for an old cripple? For I have lost everything.

AT THAT SAME TIME, THERE LAY A LAME MAN AT THE GATES.

PETER RESPONDED.

Silver and gold I do not have, but what I do have to give you is much greater.

PETER REACHED HIS HAND TOWARD THE MAN AND CLOSED HIS EYES.

In the name of Jesus Christ, walk!

I'm walking! I'm walking!

STRENGTH SURGED INTO THE MAN'S LIMBS AS HE LEAPT TO HIS FEET, AND INSTANTLY, THE LAME MAN COULD WALK.

THE MAN LEFT HIS MAT BEHIND AND WALKED WITH PETER AND JOHN THROUGH THE CITY.

WHEN THE PEOPLE SAW THE MIRACLE, THEY WERE FILLED WITH WONDER.

How?

What is this?

PETER APPROACHED A GAWKER.

Why stand there amazed? Is it so awe-inspiring that a lame man can walk or that a man can rise from the dead?

THE PEOPLE RAN TO THE HEALERS.

WHEN PETER SAW THIS,
HE ADDRESSED THEM.

Why do you stare at us?
It's not our power that
made this man walk.

The God of Abraham, Isaac,
and Jacob, the one true God
of our fathers, has glorified
his servant Jesus.

By faith in the name
of Jesus, this man
whom you see was made
strong. It is his
faith in Jesus that
has healed him.

YOU ARE THE HEIRS OF THE COVENANT OF GOD. THE COVENANT HAS BEEN OFFERED TO THE WORLD, ALL YOU HAVE TO DO IS CONFESS WITH YOUR MOUTH.

THAT DAY, THE CROWD WAS SAVED.

THE PRIESTS AND THE SADDUCEES HAD COME UP TO LISTEN TO PETER AND JOHN.

Agreed.

We cannot let this be shared.

THEY WERE GREATLY DISTURBED THAT THE APOSTLES WERE PROCLAIMING JESUS' RESURRECTION.

THEY ORDERED PETER AND JOHN TO BE SEIZED AND PUT IN JAIL.

THE NEXT DAY, THE ELDERS MET TO DISCUSS THE FATES OF PETER AND JOHN.

THE APOSTLES WERE BROUGHT FORTH FOR QUESTIONING.

By what power or what name did you perform this miracle?

Know this, it is by the name of Jesus Christ, whom you crucified, that this man was healed!

PETER WAS FILLED WITH THE HOLY SPIRIT.

Jesus is the stone you builders rejected—salvation is found in no one else. There is no other given to mankind for our forgiveness.

WHEN THEY SAW THE COURAGE OF PETER AND JOHN, THE ELDERS WERE ASTONISHED.

What are we going to do with these men?

UNSATISFIED, THE ELDERS CONFERRED TOGETHER.

The people now have seen one of Jesus' followers perform a miracle.

Bring them back in to stand before us.

213

ONCE AGAIN, PETER AND JOHN WERE BROUGHT FORTH.

We have decided that you shall not speak or teach at all in the name of Jesus.

Which is right in God's eyes: to listen to you, or to Him? You be the judge.

PETER AND JOHN REPLIED DEFIANTLY.

As for us, we cannot help speaking about what we have seen and heard.

214

Get out of here.

We never want to see you again!

AFTER FURTHER THREATS, THE SADDUCEES LET PETER AND JOHN GO.

THE SADDUCEES COMMISERATED ABOUT THEIR CONCERNS REGARDING THE MIRACLE.

PETER BRINGS THE LOVE OF CHRIST TO ALL NATIONS

Soon the Word of God will spread everywhere!

PETER TRAVELED ABOUT THE COUNTRY HEALING AND PREACHING. HE VISITED THE PEOPLE OF LYDDA.

THERE, IN LYDDA, WAS A MAN WHO HAD BEEN PARALYZED FOR YEARS.

Aeneas, Jesus Christ heals you. Get up and roll-up your mat.

217

PETER SPOKE TO THE PARALYZED MAN . . . AND THE MAN WALKED.

What is it you ask of me, Lord?

Your prayers and gifts to the poor have pleased God. Send for Peter.

A CENTURION BY THE NAME CORNELIUS WAS PRAYING TO GOD IN THE AFTERNOON WHEN AN ANGEL CAME TO HIM.

THE FOLLOWING DAY, PETER WENT UP TO THE ROOF AND PRAYED. HE SAW A VISION OF HEAVEN OPENING UP AND A LITANY OF ANIMALS DESCEND UPON THE EARTH.

Do not call anything impure that God has made.

I have come to invite you to my master's house to share the message you hold.

WHILE PETER WAS WONDERING ABOUT THE MEANING OF THE VISION, A SERVANT OF CORNELIUS CAME TO PETER.

PETER ACCEPTED THE INVITATION AND STARTED OUT TO CORNELIUS' HOUSE.

CORNELIUS CALLED ALL HIS RELATIVES AND CLOSE FRIENDS TO MEET PETER.

Stand up. I am only a man!

AT PETER'S ARRIVAL, CORNELIUS FELL TO PETER'S FEET.

Thank you for coming. We know it is against your laws.

God showed me that I should not call anyone impure or unclean! God loves all!

IT WAS AGAINST JEWISH LAW TO ASSOCIATE WITH GENTILES. YET PETER DID NOT HESITATE TO ENTER THE HOUSE OF CORNELIUS.

Why have you called for me?

Three days ago, an angel came to me. God said he had heard my prayer and remembered me. I was told to send for you.

CORNELIUS EXPLAINED WHAT HAD HAPPENED TO HIM.

I now see how true it is that God does not show favoritism, but accepts all, and nothing He has created is turned away.

PETER NOW UNDERSTOOD WHAT GOD'S MESSAGE WAS TO HIM.

WHILE PETER WAS SPEAKING, THE HOLY SPIRIT CAME TO ALL THE GENTILES IN THE ROOM.

THE JEWS WHO WERE WITH PETER WERE ASTONISHED THAT GOD HAD BLESSED GENTILES.

They are not Jews. How has this happened?

Surely no one can stand in the way of their being baptized. God loves these people just as He loves us.

PETER OVERHEARD THE NEGATIVE STATEMENTS FROM HIS JEWISH COMPANIONS.

PETER PROCEEDED TO BAPTIZE ALL WHO WERE PRESENT.

Did you hear?

It can't be so . . .

Do you think it is okay?

WORD SPREAD THROUGH THE CHRISTIAN CHURCH IN JERUSALEM THAT PETER HAD BAPTIZED GENTILES IN THE NAME OF GOD, JESUS CHRIST, AND THE HOLY SPIRIT.

I had a vision from God. It showed me that nothing is impure and unable to receive God's love.

You went into the house of uncircumcised men and ate with them. How does that make us look to other Jews?

224

WHEN PETER RETURNED TO JERUSALEM, THE BELIEVERS CRITICIZED HIM FOR HIS ACTIONS.

Then men from the Roman officer came to me. The Spirit told me to have no hesitation about going to bless and baptize them.

PETER THEN TOLD ALL THE DISCIPLES THE WHOLE STORY OF HIS PREACHING TO CORNELIUS AND HIS ASSOCIATES.

. . . And when I began to speak, the Holy Spirit came upon them. If God gave the Gentiles the gift of the Spirit, who are we to stand in the way of God?!

PETER BECAME STERN WITH THE OTHER DISCIPLES.

KING HEROD ORDERED PETER AND JAMES TO BE ARRESTED AND PUT TO DEATH.

PETER AWAITED HIS TRIAL.

THE CHURCH PRAYED FOR PETER.

AN ANGEL OF THE LORD APPEARED THAT NIGHT IN THE PRISON.

THE ANGEL OPENED THE CELL DOOR AND PETER WALKED OUT, PASSING ALL THE GUARDS UNNOTICED.

WHEN THE ANGEL AND PETER WALKED THE LENGTH OF THE STREET, THE ANGEL LEFT HIM.

PETER WENT TO THE HOUSE OF MARY, THE MOTHER OF JOHN.

It's Peter!

PETER WAS LET IN AND KEPT SAFE.

God has saved me.

THE CHURCH IS PERSECUTED

Oh no! There's always difficulties that come with progress...

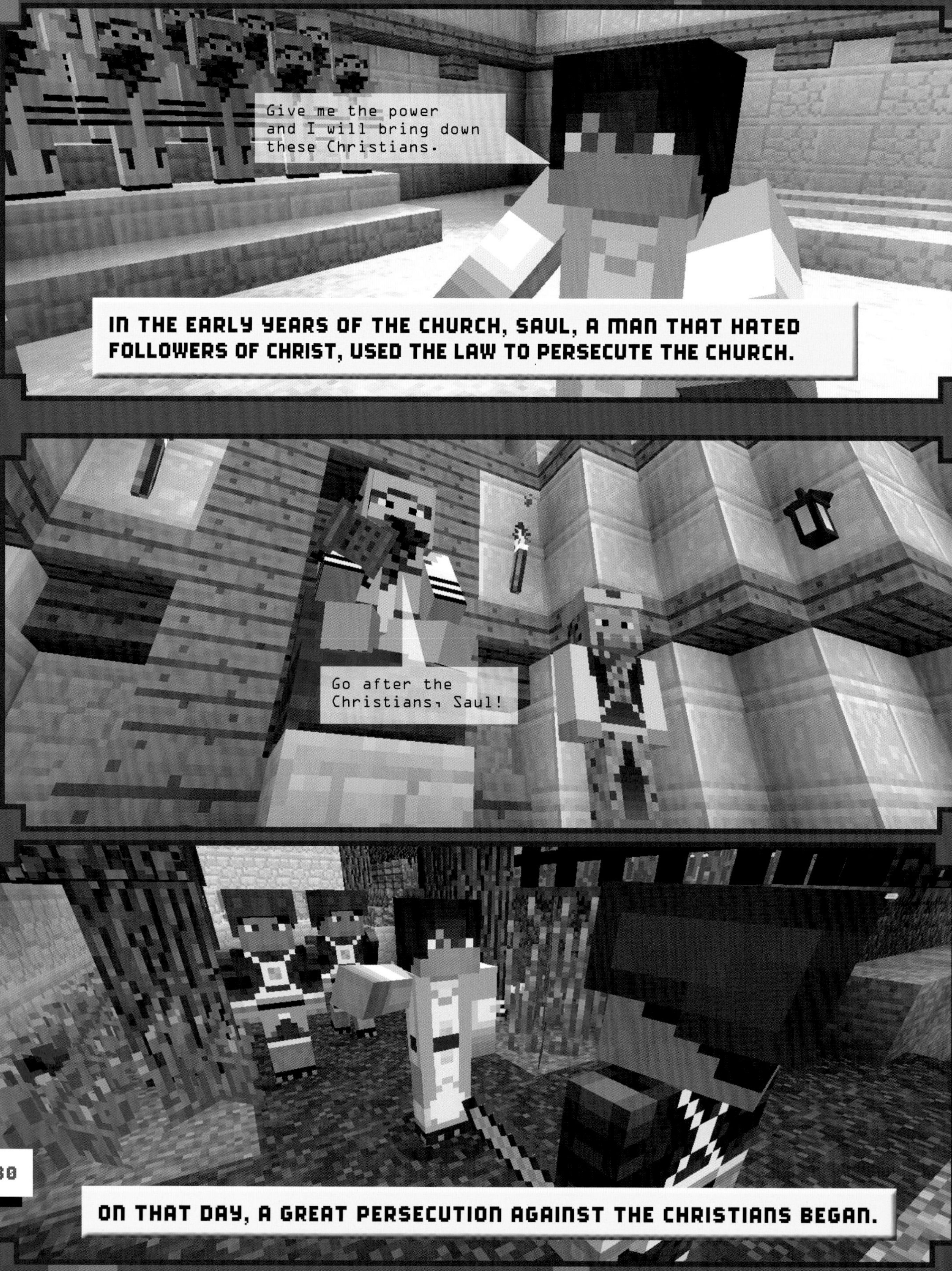
Give me the power and I will bring down these Christians.
IN THE EARLY YEARS OF THE CHURCH, SAUL, A MAN THAT HATED FOLLOWERS OF CHRIST, USED THE LAW TO PERSECUTE THE CHURCH.
Go after the Christians, Saul!
ON THAT DAY, A GREAT PERSECUTION AGAINST THE CHRISTIANS BEGAN.

SAUL WENT FROM HOUSE TO HOUSE ARRESTING ANYONE HE SUSPECTED TO BE CHRISTIAN.

EVERY CHRISTIAN WAS THROWN INTO PRISON.

THE DISCIPLES, WHO HAD BEEN SCATTERED, PREACHED THE WORD WHEREVER THEY WENT.

PHILIP WOUND UP IN THE CITY OF SAMARIA.

In the name of Jesus, you are clean!

WHEN THE PEOPLE HEARD OF THE MIRACLES PHILIP PERFORMED, THEY RUSHED TO HEAR HIM SPEAK.

A man has just arrived in the city and has done great miracles.

AT THE TIME, THERE WAS A MAN NAMED SIMON WHO WAS A SORCERER.

No one is greater than me.

SIMON WENT DOWN TO THE DOCKS WHERE PHILIP WAS HEALING THE SICK AND LAME.

In the name of Jesus Christ, may you be healed.

My arm, it is healed!

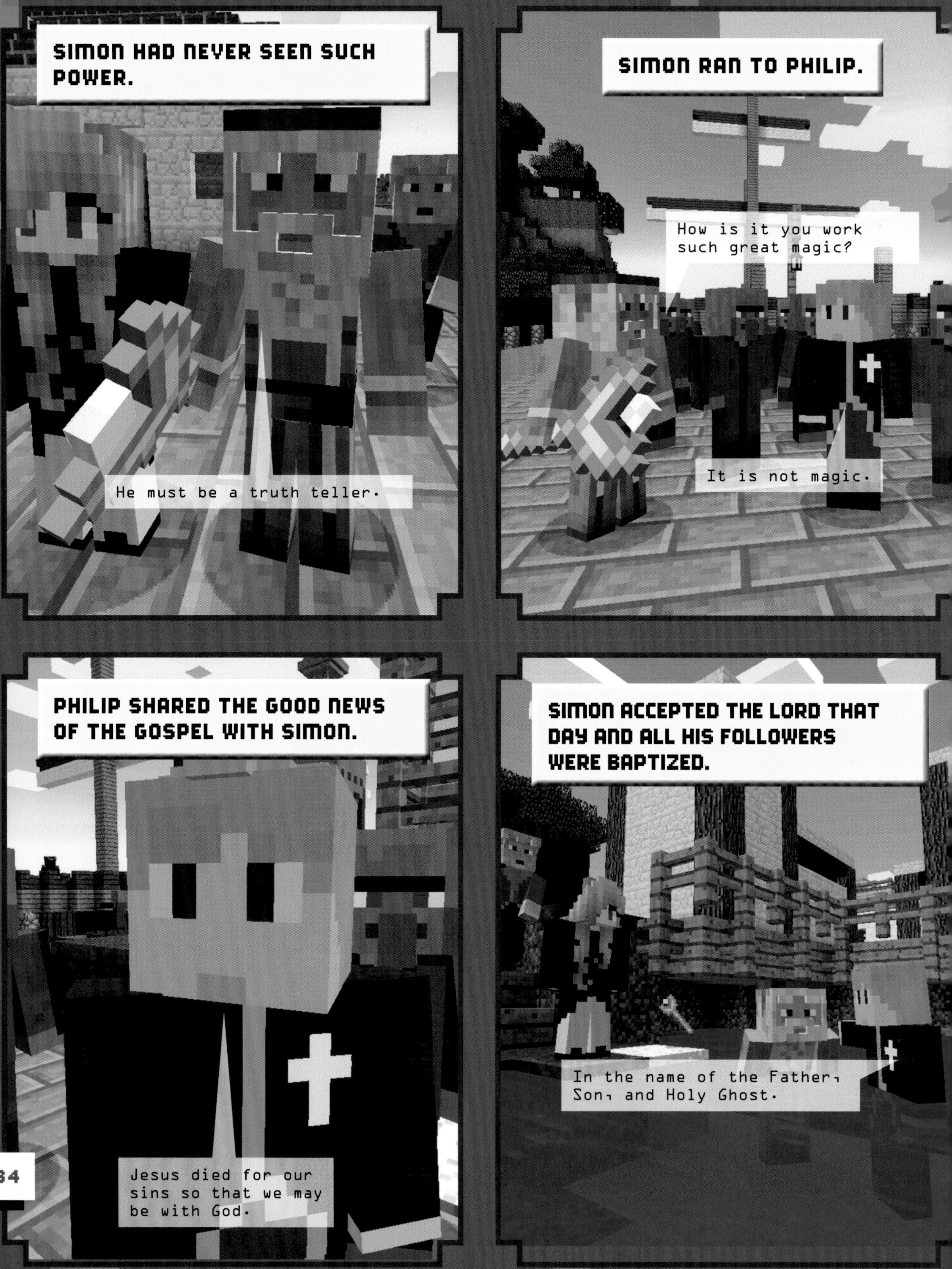
SIMON HAD NEVER SEEN SUCH POWER.
He must be a truth teller.
SIMON RAN TO PHILIP.
How is it you work such great magic?
It is not magic.
PHILIP SHARED THE GOOD NEWS OF THE GOSPEL WITH SIMON.
Jesus died for our sins so that we may be with God.
SIMON ACCEPTED THE LORD THAT DAY AND ALL HIS FOLLOWERS WERE BAPTIZED.
In the name of the Father, Son, and Holy Ghost.

SHORTLY THEREAFTER, AN ANGEL OF THE LORD CAME TO PHILIP.

Go south to the road and you will meet a man. You will know what to do when you get there.

PHILIP STARTED DOWN THE ROAD AND MET AN ETHIOPIAN.

THE ETHIOPIAN WAS READING THE BOOK OF ISAIAH.

Do you understand what this scripture means?

THE ETHIOPIAN WAS READING ABOUT THE PROPHECY OF JESUS' SACRIFICE.

PHILIP BEGAN WITH THAT PASSAGE OF SCRIPTURE THE ETHIOPIAN WAS READING, AND TOLD HIM THE STORY OF JESUS.

I wish to be baptized. Is that possible?

AFTERWARDS, THEY TRAVELED ALONG THE ROAD AND CAME TO SOME WATER.

PHILIP AND THE ETHIOPIAN WENT DOWN INTO THE WATER AND PHILIP BAPTIZED HIM IN THE NAME OF THE LORD.

SAUL'S CONVERSION

I've heard about St. Paul . . . but didn't realize he used to be Saul!

MEANWHILE, SAUL CONTINUED TO SPAT HATE AND LIBEL AGAINST THE LORD'S DISCIPLES. HE WENT TO THE HIGH PRIEST TO TAKE MATTERS TO THE NEXT LEVEL.

Yes, go and stop them.

Give me permission to go throughout Israel to arrest Christians like I did in Jerusalem. For their faith is spreading.

Saul, why do you persecute me?

SAUL TOOK THE ROAD DOWN TO DAMASCUS. ON THE ROAD, SUDDENLY A LIGHT FROM HEAVEN FLASHED AND SAUL WAS KNOCKED TO THE GROUND.

I am Jesus, whom you are persecuting. Now go into the town, and you will be told what you must do to repent for your sins.

Who are you? Who calls out to me?

SAUL GOT UP FROM THE GROUND, BUT HE COULD NO LONGER SEE.

Ananias! Go to a man named Saul. He has seen a vision that shows you coming and restoring his sight.

IN DAMASCUS, THERE WAS A DISCIPLE NAMED ANANIAS. THE LORD CALLED TO HIM IN A VISION.

Lord, I have heard of this man. He does harm to your followers.

Go! This man is my chosen instrument to proclaim my name to the kingdoms of the world. Who better to deliver my message than an adversary who has repented?

My eyesight is beginning to return!

The Lord, Jesus, who appeared to you on the road, has sent me so that you may see and be filled with the Holy Spirit.

THEN ANANIAS WENT TO THE HOUSE THAT SAUL WAS AT, AND PLACED HIS HANDS ON SAUL.

Is that Saul?

SAUL ROSE TO HIS FEET AND WAS FILLED WITH THE HOLY SPIRIT.
HE WAS BAPTIZED THAT VERY DAY.

Hey guys! You are not
going to believe this.

SAUL WAS BROUGHT TO THE DISCIPLES. THEY WERE SHOCKED.

To prove to you my faith, I will
go to the one place you are afraid
to go and proclaim the name of
Jesus.

SAUL TOLD THE DISCIPLES EVERYTHING THAT HAD HAPPENED
TO HIM, THEN ADDED ONE MORE THING.

God sent his only son to die for our sins.

AT ONCE, SAUL WENT TO THE SYNAGOGUE AND PREACHED THAT JESUS IS THE SON OF GOD.

Isn't that the man who raised havoc in Jerusalem against the Christians?

ALL WHO HEARD HIM WERE ASTONISHED.

We will watch the gate for him and get him when he goes out.

AFTER SOME TIME, THERE WAS A CONSPIRACY AMONG THE JEWS TO KILL SAUL.

Well, you have proven yourself, let us help you.

I want to be a disciple of Jesus.

MEN CAME TO KILL SAUL, SO HIS FOLLOWERS ARRIVED AT NIGHT TO HELP HIM. THEY LOWERED HIM IN A BASKET FROM THE TOP OF THE WALL AND HE ESCAPED.

SAUL WENT BACK TO JERUSALEM.

It's Saul! Don't let him in!

Barnabas, you saw my works. Take me to the disciples and tell them I am with Jesus now.

SAUL COULD NOT JOIN THE DISCIPLES ON HIS OWN, SO HE WENT TO A MAN NAMED BARNABAS.

SAUL TRIED TO JOIN THE DISCIPLES IN JERUSALEM, BUT THEY WERE AFRAID OF HIM.

SO BARNABAS TOOK SAUL TO PETER AND TOLD THEM HOW SAUL HAD SEEN JESUS AND ACCEPTED HIM INTO HIS HEART.

AFTER THAT, SAUL STAYED WITH THEM AND PREACHED BOLDLY IN THE MARKET SQUARES OF JERUSALEM.

SAUL GOES TO THE GENTILES AND GETS A NEW NAME

Here comes Paul!

BARNABAS AND SAUL WERE SENT ON THEIR WAY
BY THE HOLY SPIRIT TO SAIL TO CYPRUS.

WHEN THEY ARRIVED AT CYPRUS, THEY PROCLAIMED THE WORD
OF GOD IN THE LOCAL SYNAGOGUE. PEOPLE CAME TO KNOW
SAUL BECAUSE OF HIS ROUSING LECTURES.

My master, Sergius Paulus, the proconsul of the island, wishes to meet you.

We would be happy to meet your master.

THEY TRAVELED THROUGH THE WHOLE ISLAND AND EVENTUALLY CAME TO PAPHOS, WHERE THEY MET A JEWISH SORCERER AND FALSE PROPHET NAMED BAR-JESUS.

Master, they are here as you ask, but they preach lies and false truths. Do not take them into your house.

Peace to you, Bar-Jesus, but I wish to speak to the men. Let them in.

BAR-JESUS OPPOSED SAUL AND TRIED TO TURN THE PROCONSUL FROM THE FAITH.

You are a child of the Devil and an enemy of everything that is right. You are filled with deceit and tricks. Will you ever stop perverting God's word? For your sin, you will be blind for a time because you caused so many to be blind to God.

WHEN SAUL CAME IN, HE FIRST ADDRESSED BAR-JESUS.

Please, servant of the living God, show mercy on me! I have been led astray, but not by my own doing.

Rise to your feet. It is by your own tongue you can ask for mercy from God. Pray in the name of Jesus to be forgiven.

IMMEDIATELY BAR-JESUS WENT BLIND. WHEN THE PROCONSUL SAW THIS, HE FELL AT SAUL'S FEET.

ON THE SABBATH, SAUL ENTERED THE PATHOS SYNAGOGUE. THE LEADERS ASKED HIM TO SPEAK ABOUT JESUS.

Therefore, my friend, I want you to know that through Jesus, forgiveness of sins are proclaimed to you.

Thank you for sharing this great news with us.

We would love to have you come again and speak more about this Jesus.

AS SAUL AND BARNABAS WERE LEAVING THE SYNAGOGUE, THE PEOPLE INVITED THEM TO SPEAK FURTHER ABOUT JESUS ON THE NEXT SABBATH.

ON THE NEXT SABBATH, ALMOST THE WHOLE CITY GATHERED TO HEAR THE WORD OF THE LORD.

Saul tells lies. I wouldn't listen to him.

God is only for the Jews.

There never was a man named Jesus.

WHEN THE JEWISH LEADERSHIP SAW THE CROWD, THEY WERE FILLED WITH JEALOUSY AND FEAR. THEY BEGAN TO CONTRADICT WHAT SAUL SAID.

We had to speak the word of God to you first. Since you reject it and do not consider yourselves worthy of eternal life, we now turn to the Gentiles.

WHEN THEY CAME TO RENOUNCE SAUL, HE RESPONDED BOLDLY.

We are calling you our apostle. The Gentile word for Saul is Paul. You are our apostle Paul.

I shall take the title with joy and gratitude.

THE GENTILES WERE GLAD AND HUMBLED THE WORD OF THE LORD WAS BROUGHT TO THEM. THEY GAVE SAUL A NEW NAME.

THE JEWISH LEADERS, NOW FURIOUS AT PAUL, INCITED THE WOMEN AGAINST HIM. THEY STIRRED UP PERSECUTION, AND PAUL WAS EXPELLED FROM THE CITY.

FRUSTRATED ABOUT HIS EXPULSION, PAUL SHOOK THE DUST OFF HIS FEET BEFORE HE LEFT AS A WARNING TO THEM AND HEADED TO THE NEXT TOWN.

PAUL'S FIRST HEALING

Now Paul can really begin
Jesus' work.

PAUL JOURNEYED WITH BARNABAS TO THE TOWN OF LYSTRA TO CONTINUE HIS WORK WITH THE GENTILES. THERE SAT A MAN WHO HAD BEEN CRIPPLED FROM BIRTH.

I see you have great love for the Lord and believe in what I tell you. So, in the name of Jesus, stand up on your feet!

I love God and have faith that I will be healed.

PAUL PREACHED TO THE MAN, AND AS HE WAS SHARING THE STORY OF JESUS, PAUL SAW THE FAITH OF THE MAN SHINE THROUGH.

AT THAT, THE MAN ROSE AND LEAPT IN THE AIR.

Hermes has come to us.

Praise the gods!

He is Zeus!

WHEN THE CROWD SAW WHAT PAUL HAD DONE, THEY SHOUTED PRAISE, CALLING PAUL AND BARNABAS GODS.

Friends, we, too, are only human.
We come to bring you good news.
Turn away from those lies and
toward the one living God.

BUT WHEN THE APOSTLES HEARD THIS, THEY REJECTED THE CLAIMS.

They tell you they are men, so it
is the Devil who gives them power.

**BEFORE PAUL COULD TEACH THE CROWD, SOME JEWS
FROM ANTIOCH ATTACKED AND THREW STONES AT HIM.**

A QUESTION FROM THE GENTILES

What about saving the Gentiles?

PAUL FLED FOR ANTIOCH. BARNABUS HEADED BACK TO JERUSALEM.

You cannot be saved unless you follow all of Moses' laws, so Gentiles must follow our laws.

I disagree.

AS HE ENTERED THE NEW CITY, PAUL CAME UPON AN ARGUMENT BETWEEN TWO BELIEVERS.

Paul, you are close to the apostles. Will you take our question to them?

I just got here, but sure. I will head back to Jerusalem for you.

THEY APPOINTED PAUL TO SPEAK WITH THE APOSTLES AND ELDERS ABOUT THIS QUESTION.

WHEN PAUL CAME TO JERUSALEM, HE WAS WELCOMED BY THE CHURCH AND THE APOSTLES AND ELDERS. HE WAS BROUGHT TO A MEETING HALL WHERE HE PRESENTED THE QUESTION.

The Gentiles must be circumcised and required to keep the laws of Moses.

SOME OF THE BELIEVERS WHO BELONGED TO THE PARTY OF THE PHARISEES STOOD UP AND VOICED THEIR OPINION.

Brothers, you know that God chose that Gentiles should hear the "Good News" and believe.

THEN APOSTLES AND THE ELDERS MET TO CONSIDER THE ISSUE. AFTER MUCH DISCUSSION, PETER ADDRESSED ALL OF THEM.

God who knows the heart and accepted them just as they were. Who are we to discriminate if they do not keep all the laws?

It is my judgement that we should not make it difficult for Gentiles to turn to God.

Instead, we will write to the Gentile believers, telling them to abstain from food polluted by idols and from evil relationships.

THEN, THE APOSTLES AND ELDERS SENT PAUL AND BARNABAS OUT TO THE GENTILES WITH THEIR ANSWER.

Let us go back and visit all the believers in the towns we preached.

Great, let's go. I want to take Mark with us.

EVEN GREAT FRIENDSHIPS HAVE THEIR DIFFICULTIES, AND PAUL AND BARNABAS HAD QUITE A DISAGREEMENT.

But Mark deserted us and did not help us with our works. He is not coming with us and that is that!

I don't care. He has changed and we are close friends now. He will come or I will leave.

Then leave.

THEY HAD SUCH A SHARP DISAGREEMENT THAT THEY PARTED COMPANY. BARNABAS TOOK MARK AND SAILED TO CYPRUS.

PAUL PREACHES
TO THE GREEKS

Lord, has the time come for the Greeks to hear the message of Jesus? Who will you send to them?

PAUL AND SILAS TRAVELED DOWN TO TROAS.

Come over to Macedonia and help us.

DURING THE NIGHT, PAUL HAD A VISION OF A MAN OF MACEDONIA STANDING AND BEGGING HIM.

My brother, the Holy Spirit has given me a vision: we must go to Macedonia.

OK. I'm in.

PAUL WOKE AND SPOKE TO SILAS ABOUT HIS VISION.

We have a change of plans. We would like to head to Philippi.

You're in luck. That is our next port. Stay on and I will take you there.

FROM TROAS, PAUL AND SILAS HEADED TO PHILIPPI, THE ROMAN COLONY, IN THE DISTRICT OF MACEDONIA.

ON THE FIRST SABBATH UPON THEIR ARRIVAL, PAUL AND SILAS WENT OUTSIDE THE CITY TO THE RIVER TO FIND A PLACE TO PRAY.

AS THEY WALKED, THEY CAME UPON SEVERAL WOMEN WHO WERE THERE HAVING A PICNIC.

. . . And so he died for our sins.

My name is Lydia, and I am a simple cloth dealer. My heart has opened up to your message.

PAUL AND SILAS APPROACHED AND BEGAN TO SPEAK TO THE WOMEN WHO HAD GATHERED THERE. THESE WOMEN BECAME SOME OF THE FIRST GREEK CHRISTIANS.

ONE DAY, WHILE STAYING IN PHILIPPI, PAUL WENT TO THE MARKET WHERE HE MET A FEMALE SLAVE WHO HAD EVIL SPIRITS IN HER.

Are you going to save people with your mighty God?

Please leave me alone. If you do not want to hear the message, then be on your way.

THE NEXT DAY, THE FORTUNE-TELLER MET PAUL ON HIS MORNING WALK TO GO PREACH. SHE BEGAN TO MOCK HIM.

No God is more powerful than me! Even you, little man, cannot tell the future. I can! So I am greater than you!

THOUGH PAUL ASKED TO BE LEFT ALONE, THE FORTUNE-TELLER FOLLOWED HIM. THE EVIL SPIRIT INSIDE HER SPOKE THROUGH HER.

SHE FOLLOWED PAUL AROUND THE MARKET MOCKING HIM AGAIN AND AGAIN.

SHE KEPT THIS UP FOR MANY DAYS. FINALLY, PAUL BECAME SO ANNOYED THAT HE TURNED AROUND AND CAST THE EVIL SPIRIT OUT OF THE FORTUNE-TELLER.

These men are Jews, and are throwing the city into an uproar by practicing customs unlawful to Romans.

THE EVIL SPIRIT HAD HELPED THE WOMAN TELL THE FUTURE AND MAKE MONEY. WHEN HER OWNERS REALIZED THAT THEIR HOPE OF MAKING MONEY WAS GONE, THEY SEIZED PAUL AND SILAS, DRAGGING THEM INTO THE MARKETPLACE TO FACE THE AUTHORITIES.

THE CROWD JOINED IN, AND THE MAGISTRATE ORDERED THEM BEATEN AND THROWN INTO PRISON.

Jailer, I command you
to guard these men
carefully or it will
be your life.

Yes, I understand.

Lord, please bless
those who hold us, so
that they remain in
your will.

**RATHER THAN BEING ANGRY, PAUL AND SILAS BEGAN SINGING
HYMNS TO GOD AND PRAYED FOR THE GUARD.**

How strange. They pray
for me and show love
to me, even though I
am their enemy.

271

AT ABOUT MIDNIGHT, GOD SHOOK THE EARTH AND THE PRISON WITH HIS MIGHTY PRESENCE. AT ONCE, ALL THE DOORS FLEW OPEN AND EVERYONE'S CHAINS CAME LOOSE. THE GUARD, TRAPPED IN HIS ROOM, FINALLY FREED HIMSELF TO FIND ALL THE PRISON DOORS OPEN—TOO LATE TO STOP ANY FROM ESCAPING.

HE DREW HIS SWORD AND WAS READY TO END HIS LIFE, FOR HE KNEW HIS FATE FROM THE MAGISTRATE.

Don't harm yourself. We are still here!

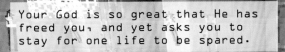

♪ Your God is so great that He has freed you, and yet asks you to stay for one life to be spared.

We both stayed because we knew your life depended on it.

THE GUARD RUSHED IN AND FELL TREMBLING BEFORE PAUL AND SILAS.

Sirs, what must I do to be saved?

Believe in the Lord Jesus, and you will be saved.

THE GUARD THEN BROUGHT THEM OUT AND ASKED THEM TO SHARE GOD WITH HIM.

THAT VERY HOUR, THE GUARD TOOK PAUL AND SILAS TO HIS HOUSE WHERE HE WASHED THEIR WOUNDS WHILE PAUL SHARED GOD'S STORY.

AFTER PAUL AND SILAS HAD BAPTIZED THE JAILER AND HIS WHOLE FAMILY, THEY BROKE BREAD TOGETHER, JUST AS JESUS HAD TAUGHT HIS FOLLOWERS TO DO IN MEMORY OF HIS SACRIFICE.

The Magistrate gave orders to release you. You can leave now. Go in peace, my brothers.

WHEN IT WAS DAYLIGHT, THE MAGISTRATE SENT ORDERS TO THE JAILER TO RELEASE PAUL AND SILAS.

They beat us publicly without trial, even though we are Roman citizens, and then threw us into prison. No, we will not leave quietly. Let the Magistrate come and escort us out of the city. Take this message to your master.

Please, my brothers! This is your chance to escape. Leave while you can.

No, we preach only peace and love, and for that, we are called evil. We heal the sick, and for that we are beaten.

What am I to do? These men are Roman citizens. If they report me to Rome for what I have done, I will lose my life.

You'd better beg for forgiveness.

WHEN THE MESSENGER TOLD THE MAGISTRATE ALL THAT PAUL HAD SAID, THE MAGISTRATE BECAME VERY AFRAID.

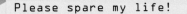

Please spare my life!

I was commanded to love my enemy, so I hold nothing against you. May Jesus' mercy be upon you.

You forgive him? Truly, your God is the greatest!

THE MAGISTRATE CAME BEFORE PAUL AND BEGGED FOR FORGIVENESS.

Forgive him? Why? I thought you went there to humiliate him.

My heart is filled with love. One who loves can only forgive. The Lord will give us justice in this life or the next! Now I will go in peace.

LATER, THE JAILER QUESTIONED PAUL.

Praise your faith and will to follow Jesus' example. Remember, Jesus said, "Do unto others, as you want them to do unto you."

Truly, you are a speaker of truth. You live by what you preach, and I will follow in the example you set.

THE JAILER WAS AMAZED AT THE LOVE AND MERCY THAT PAUL HAD SHOWN.

SHORTLY AFTER, PAUL AND SILAS PACKED UP THEIR THINGS AND LEFT TO CONTINUE THEIR WORKS IN SPREADING THE MESSAGE OF JESUS AND GROWING THE CHURCH IN GREECE.

THE PERSECUTION
OF PAUL

Poor Paul!

WHEN PAUL AND HIS COMPANION HAD PASSED THROUGH AMPHIPOLIS AND APOLLONIA, THEY CAME TO THESSALONICA, WHERE THERE WAS A JEWISH SYNAGOGUE. AS WAS HIS CUSTOM, PAUL WENT INTO THE SYNAGOGUE.

Jesus, I am proclaiming, fulfilled these scriptures.

FOR THREE SABBATHS, PAUL REASONED, THROUGH SCRIPTURE, THAT JESUS HAD TO SUFFER AND RISE FROM THE DEAD.

SOME OF THE JEWS WERE NOT PERSUADED, BUT A LARGE NUMBER OF GREEKS BECAME BELIEVERS.

God can love even a Gentile like me?

Yes, God's new covenant is that with those who believe.

Form a mob and riot.

It's going to cost you!

THE JEWS BECAME JEALOUS THAT GOD WOULD SHARE HIS GRACE AND BLESSINGS WITH GENTILES, SO THEY ROUNDED UP BAD CHARACTERS TO HURT PAUL.

A MOB FORMED, AND THEY RUSHED TO THE MAN'S HOUSE WHERE PAUL AND SILAS WERE STAYING.

WHEN THEY ARRIVED, HOWEVER, THEY DID NOT FIND PAUL. INSTEAD, THE MOB DRAGGED JASON, THE MAN SHELTERING PAUL, BEFORE THE CITY OFFICIALS.

These men who have caused trouble all over are here now in our
city! Jason has welcomed them
into his house.

We need to go before the
courts. Jason cannot take
the blame for us.

It is too dangerous!
Jason will only have
to pay a fine. You,
they'll stone!

WHILE JASON STOOD BEFORE THE COURT, PAUL AND SILAS HID.

Preaching one's religion is not a crime against Caesar, but to keep the peace, I will fine this man for hosting these preachers.

They say that their Jesus is ruling over all. They are defying Caesar's decrees!

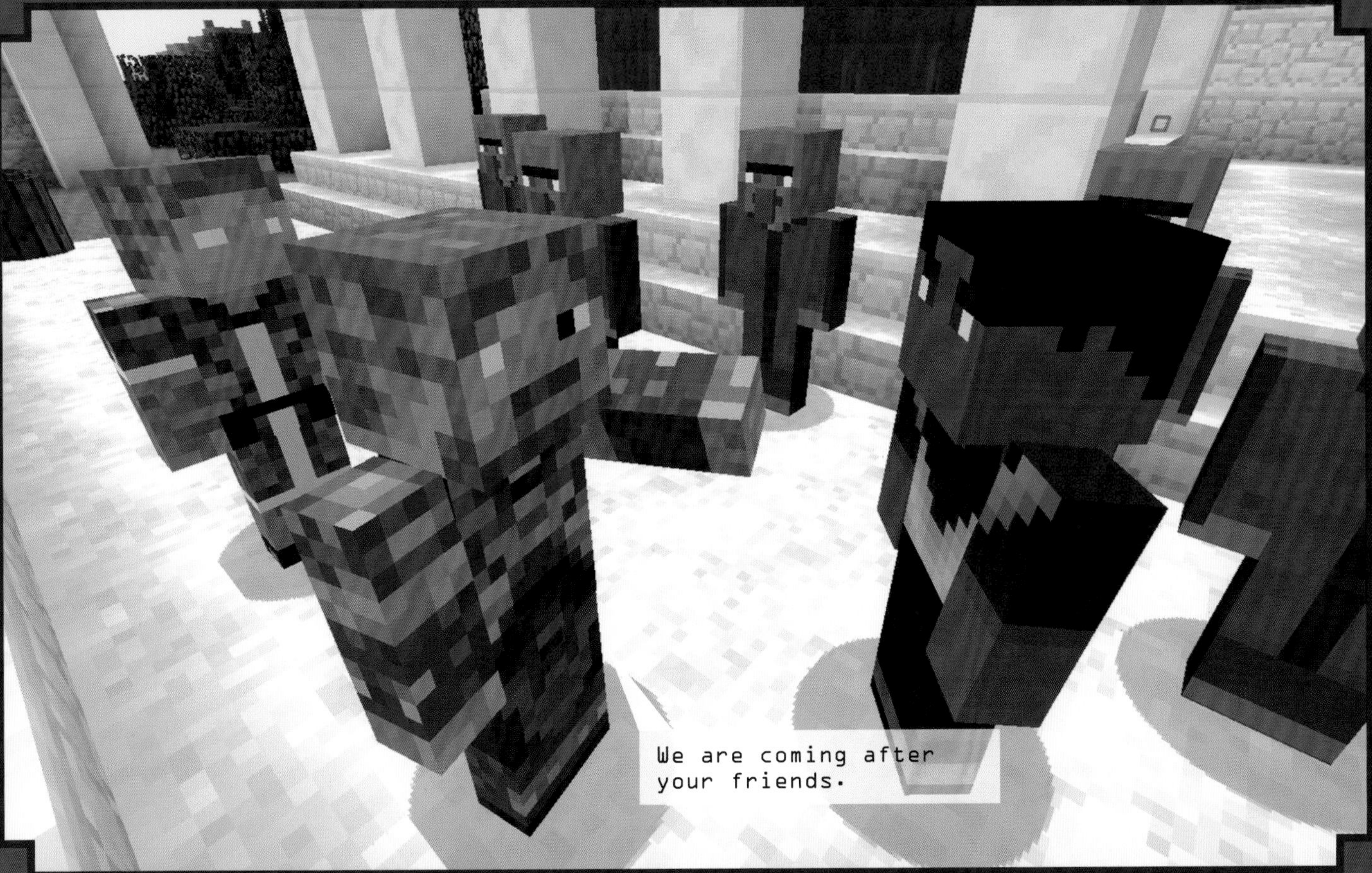
We are coming after your friends.

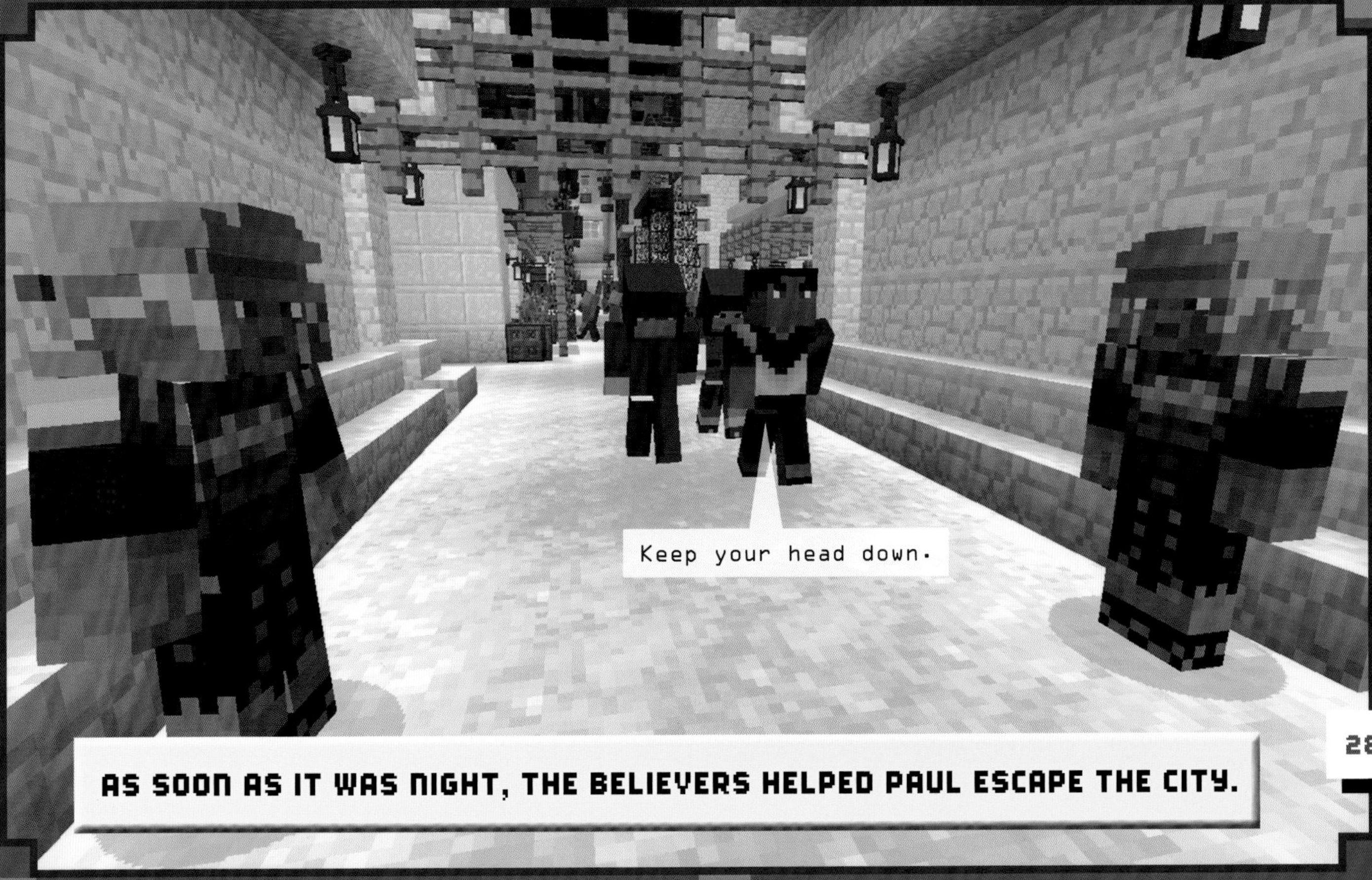
Keep your head down.
AS SOON AS IT WAS NIGHT, THE BELIEVERS HELPED PAUL ESCAPE THE CITY.

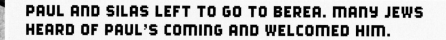

PAUL AND SILAS LEFT TO GO TO BEREA. MANY JEWS HEARD OF PAUL'S COMING AND WELCOMED HIM.

Jesus claimed to be the "I am" of Daniel.

He forgave sins?

He rose from the dead?

THE PEOPLE OF BEREA RECEIVED THE MESSAGE WITH GREAT EAGERNESS, STUDYING THE SCRIPTURE EVERY DAY TO SEE IF WHAT PAUL SAID WAS TRUE.

We must go to Berea and agitate the people against Paul.

Yes, let us go and stir up trouble.

THOSE WHO STOOD AGAINST CHRIST RECEIVED A MESSAGE THAT PAUL WAS PREACHING IN BEREA.

Paul, the people have turned. You need to leave.

287

THE PEOPLE OF BEREA TURNED AGAINST THE BELIEVERS.

THE BELIEVERS IMMEDIATELY TOOK PAUL TO THE COAST.

THEY BROUGHT PAUL TO ATHENS AND LEFT WITH INSTRUCTIONS FOR SILAS TO JOIN HIM WHEN POSSIBLE.

Take this letter back with you and give it to Silas.

WHILE WAITING IN ATHENS, PAUL WAS GREATLY DISTRESSED TO SEE THAT THE CITY WAS FULL OF IDOLS.

PAUL PREACHED IN THE MARKET-PLACE TO THOSE WHO HAPPENED TO BE THERE.

To an Unknown God

You are bringing some strange ideas to our ears. We would like to know who this God you speak of is.

A GROUP OF PHILOSOPHERS BEGAN TO DEBATE HIM.

To an Unknown God

I walked around and looked carefully at your objects of worship.

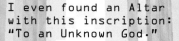

I even found an Altar with this inscription: "To an Unknown God."

So you are ignorant of the very thing you worship, and this is what I am going to proclaim to you: This is the God I speak of. Yet He is not served by human hands. Rather, He Himself gives to everyone alike and all things . . .

He marked you out with an appointed time in history. God did this so that you would seek Him. For in Him, we live. Therefore, since we are like God and His offspring, do not think of Him as stone to worship an image. For He has set the day of judgement with justice through one man, who gave his life as the only begotten son. Whoever shall believe in Him will not perish, but rather, will have eternal life!

AFTER PREACHING IN ATHENS FOR A TIME, PAUL LEFT AND WENT TO CORINTH.

THERE, PAUL MET A JEWISH MAN NAMED AQUILA WHO HAD RECENTLY COME FROM ROME.

Claudius Caesar has ordered all Jews to leave Rome.

That's terrible to hear.

AQUILA WAS A TENTMAKER, AND PAUL STAYED AND WORKED WITH HIM.

So why leave Athens?

The people did not receive the word and soon turned on me.

That is terrible. Do you feel like giving up?

Yes, I have not had much success of late in my work of sharing the Gospel . . . but if it will save one person, then it is worth the effort. So I keep going.

PAUL ARRESTED AND SHIPWRECKED

Now a shipwreck?!

AFTER A SHORT TIME OF PEACE, PAUL PICKED HIMSELF UP AND RETURNED TO JERUSALEM TO START UP HIS MINISTRY AGAIN.

WHEN PAUL ARRIVED IN JERUSALEM, HE WENT AND PRESENTED HIMSELF TO JAMES AND THE ELDERS, REPORTING ALL THE WORK HE HAD DONE WITH THE GENTILES.

They have been informed that you teach Jews who live among Gentiles to turn away from Moses.

PAUL WAS WARNED BY JAMES THAT THOSE WHO WERE ZEALOUS FOR THE LAW HAD TURNED ON HIM.

They will have certainly heard that you are in Jerusalem. To save your life, you must do what we tell you.

Take these men, join in their purification rites.

WHEN THE SEVEN DAYS OF PURIFICATION WERE NEARLY OVER, PAUL WAS SEEN AT THE TEMPLE. THOSE THERE STIRRED UP THE CROWD AND PAUL WAS SEIZED.

THE PEOPLE DRAGGED PAUL TO THE CITY GATES.

Gather the troops.

NEWS REACHED THE ROMAN COMMANDER
THAT THE WHOLE CITY WAS IN AN UPROAR.

Form-up!

THE COMMANDER, AT ONCE, READIED HIS TROOPS.

THE COMMANDER AND HIS SOLDIERS MARCHED TOWARD THE GATES.

You're under arrest.

Me? I am innocent and was attacked for what I believe.

Well, this is mob rule by these people, so you're under arrest in order to quell the mob.

THE RIOTERS SCATTERED WHEN THEY SAW THE SOLDIERS, LEAVING PAUL ALONE IN THE STREET.

Commander, I am a citizen of no ordinary city, Rome! I think you have heard of it. I wish to be held on trial in Rome, which is my right.

I understand. I will make arrangements and you will be out of my hair.

299

WHEN IT WAS DECIDED THAT PAUL WOULD SAIL TO ITALY, HE AND SOME OTHER PRISONERS WERE BROUGHT TO THE WHARF AND HANDED OVER TO A CENTURION.

THEY BOARDED THE SHIP AND SET SAIL ALONG THE COAST, THEN OUT TO OPEN SEA.

Storm on the horizon, Captain.

BEFORE LONG, OMINOUS CLOUDS WERE SIGHTED IN THE SHIP'S PATH.

Our draft is too deep! We need to shed weight! Throw everything we can overboard!

IN A TORRENT OF RAGE, A HURRICANE WAS SOON DEVOURING THE SHIP, SENDING IT HURTLING TOWARDS A SHALLOW REEF.

I stand beside you! Do not be afraid. For God has told me that only the ship will be destroyed. You all shall be spared by God.

WHEN ALL HOPE WAS LOST, PAUL CAME UP TO SPEAK TO THE CREW.

JUST AS PAUL HAD SPOKEN HIS WORDS, THE SHIP RAN AGROUND AND SPLINTERED TO PIECES, BUT ALL THE MEN WERE WASHED UP ON SHORE ALIVE.

THE MEN STARTED A FIRE DESPITE THE COLD AND RAIN, BUT THEY NEEDED DRY WOOD TO KEEP IT GOING.

PAUL WENT TO GATHER WOOD, AND AS HE PUT HIS HAND TO THE GROUND, A VIPER STRUCK HIM.

Only God can save him.

He will surely die.

That is a viper bite.

PAUL RETURNED AND EXPLAINED WHAT HAD HAPPENED, THUS THE OTHERS BELIEVED HIM DOOMED.

Look, nothing can hurt this man, because he believes in the one true God!

Please teach us about Jesus.

THE SAILORS EXPECTED HIM TO SWELL UP OR FALL DEAD DURING THE NIGHT, BUT COME MORNING, PAUL STOOD AT THE FIRE AS IF NOTHING HAD HAPPENED.

WITH THE PASSING OF THE STORM—AND PAUL MIRACULOUSLY BEING HEALED—THE MEN SET OFF TO EXPLORE THE ISLAND WHICH HELD THEM CAPTIVE. GUIDED BY THE HOLY SPIRIT, THEY CAME TO A NEARBY ESTATE THAT BELONGED TO THE CHIEF OFFICIAL OF THE ISLAND.

Welcome to my home. You are welcome to stay as long as you need. I must apologize, however, for I cannot attend to your needs, as my father is very sick.

Thank you. Please, may I see your father and pray for him, in return for your kindness?

THE CHIEF OFFICIAL WELCOMED PAUL TO HIS HOUSE.

In the name of Jesus, our loving Lord, heal this man.

THE OLD MAN'S FEVER RAGED ON WITH NO SIGN OF BREAKING. PAUL WENT IN AND PRAYED, PLACING HIS HANDS ON HIM, AND IN MOMENTS, HE WAS HEALED.

NEWS OF THE HEALING SPREAD QUICKLY, AND SOON, THE REMAINDER OF THE SICK ON THE ISLAND CAME AND WERE CURED BY THE LORD.

AFTER THREE MONTHS, PAUL PUT OUT TO SEA WITH HIS ROMAN GUARDS TO GO BACK TO ROME.

SOON, HE RETURNED TO THE MAJESTIC CAPITAL OF THE EMPIRE.

Praise the Lord, Paul has reached Rome.

THE BROTHERS AND SISTERS OF THE FAITH HEARD THAT PAUL WAS IN ROME AND CAME TO SUPPORT HIM IN HIS MINISTRY.

PAUL WAS ALLOWED TO LIVE BY HIMSELF, WITH A SOLDIER TO GUARD HIM.

FOR TWO WHOLE YEARS, PAUL STAYED IN HIS RENTED HOUSE. HE PROCLAIMED THE KINGDOM OF GOD AND THE LORD JESUS CHRIST. IN TIME, THE CHURCH IN ROME GREW LARGER AND BEGAN TO SPREAD THROUGHOUT ITS MASSIVE EMPIRE.

ACKNOWLEDGMENTS

TO OUR READERS:

First of all, thank you for taking time to pick up this book. We hope that you've enjoyed reading it as much as we did making it. As middle school teachers, we have always maintained a passion for projects where we could experiment with new curriculum and teaching practices through technology. When we started the Advanced Learning Project years ago, we had no idea it would lead us down so many varied paths, starting with summer camps in robotics, rocketry, and computer building, which evolved into developing Craft-Academy, our Minecraft education platform and curriculum. We host educational Minecraft servers, and write books that take place in Minecraft worlds. We feel truly blessed that we have been given the opportunity to share our creative educational endeavors with the world.

Putting a project like this together requires a team effort, and for that, we would like to acknowledge a few people:

We wouldn't be making these books if it were not for our editor Krishan Trotman. She found us, she believed in us, and we thank her deeply for the opportunity.

Big thanks to Noppes for the support he provided us using his Custom NPCs and More Player Models 2 mods.

Thanks to our assistant developer George Higashiyama, and, of course, our students—you know who you are!